A BEAUTIFUL LOVE

A BEAUTIFUL LOVE

MEGAN WALKER

A Beautiful Love © 2019 by Megan Walker.
All Rights Reserved.

All rights reserved. No part of this book may be reproduced in any form or by any electronic or mechanical means including information storage and retrieval systems, without permission in writing from the author. The only exception is by a reviewer, who may quote short excerpts in a review.

Cover design: Blue Water Books

This book is a work of fiction. Names, characters, places, and incidents either are products of the author's imagination or are used fictitiously. Any resemblance to actual persons, living or dead, events, or locales is entirely coincidental.

Megan Walker
https://www.facebook.com/authormeganwalker

First Printing: March 2019

ALSO BY MEGAN WALKER

Lakeshire Park
A Beautiful Love
Her Unexpected Courtship

Titles in the Forever After Retellings:

Beauty and the Baron, by Joanna Barker
The Captain and Miss Winter, by Sally Britton
The Steadfast Heart by Arlem Hawks
A Beautiful Love by Megan Walker
Maiden in the Tower by Heidi Kimball

To my husband, Ted:
I always knew you were a swan.

THE UGLY DUCKLING

Then they [the children] threw more bread and cake into the water, and said, "The new one is the most beautiful of all; he is so young and pretty." And the old swans bowed their heads before him.

Then he felt quite ashamed, and hid his head under his wing; for he did not know what to do, he was so happy, and yet not at all proud. He had been persecuted and despised for his ugliness, and now he heard them say he was the most beautiful of all the birds. Even the elder-tree bent down its bows into the water before him, and the sun shone warm and bright. Then he rustled his feathers, curved his slender neck, and cried joyfully, from the depths of his heart, "I never dreamed of such happiness as this, while I was an ugly duckling."

-Hans Christian Anderson, 1844

CHAPTER 1

"Welcome back to Mayberry Park, Mr. Blake." A footman held the coach door open in anticipation.

Though Preston's mind told him to move, some invisible force glued him to his seat. He was not ready to be back at the Averys' estate. A year was too soon after all that had plagued him.

"Preston?" Mother urged with widened eyes. "Shall we?"

He sighed in response, looking out the opposite window. Instantly he saw his own reflection in the glass and squeezed his eyes shut, but in vain. Etched in his memory was a picture of tightened skin that raked across his jawline, reaching up midway to his cheek. How could he greet his lifelong friends like this? Mrs. Avery was as good as a second mother to him, and Mr. Avery a father. Thomas was the closest thing he had to a brother.

And Caroline.

Caroline was everything good about the world.

Sending her that letter a few months after his accident had taken every last bit of strength within him. Preston would rather crawl into the deepest cave than show himself to her.

How could any of the Averys ever accept him as he now was? Society certainly didn't, and the Averys were nothing if not the center of Suffolk society. "This visit was a mistake," he said.

"No. A mistake is sitting awkwardly in your carriage when your hosts are rushing out to greet you. Come now and help your mother down so she might see her dearest friends."

Preston stretched his neck and forced his leaden legs to step out of the coach. Mrs. and Mr. Avery were descending the stairs to greet them.

"Opal, Preston, how thrilled we are to have you back in our home!" Mrs. Avery rushed over to embrace Preston's mother. The two friends' instant reconnection should have made the day's journey worth it, but Preston still felt hollow.

Preston made to turn, to ensure that the servants were making good work of their bags, when he found Thomas standing only a few feet away, mouth agape, eyes set, and his entire body rigid. Preston was accustomed to such stares from the occasional errands he had attempted in town. The discomfort of others had become his burden to carry, his responsibility to quell. He'd rehearsed a million times the jokes he'd make with Thomas when they were finally face to face once more. "I'll always win most heroic bachelor," he'd say, and Thomas would scowl in jest.

Instead, Preston's stomach sank at the stare his oldest friend could not hide. Thomas took a few slow steps closer, averting his eyes and frowning as though thinking of something, anything to say.

This trip had been a mistake indeed.

"We're so glad you've come," Thomas said as he approached. "How're you feeling, Blake?"

"Not as wretched as I look."

Thomas braved a glance at Preston's cheek, but then quickly brought his eyes back, meeting Preston's straight on. His expression was worried, as though he'd already said something offensive.

Preston tried again. "I am well. Recovery has been long and I cannot say I enjoyed laying in bed for half the year. And of course, these scars still take getting used to."

"It's not . . . really, it's not that bad." Thomas rubbed his chin and cleared his throat. "And what you did for that family . . ."

"It is what it is," Preston said. It was his turn to look away.

He knew Mayberry Park well after spending a month every summer there in his childhood, and then some. He'd missed his friends. The Averys and the Blakes shared a long history of friendship. Despite everything, there was still a feeling of homecoming as his eyes took in the loft height of the stone house surrounded by acres and acres of green. A million memories to relive.

Just this time last year he'd been with Caroline. His heart dropped remembering her easy smile, the vibrant way she looked at him when they snuck off to venture around the estate. He'd meant to keep his promises to her. Every last one. But, now? There was nothing left of him to give.

At least he still had Thomas. "When did you return from your tour?" Preston asked.

"A month or so after your accident. I wanted to visit, but Mama said you preferred we stayed away."

"Well, if you think this is bad," Preston motioned to his scars, "you wouldn't have stomached the beginning of it." Thomas had always been the type to squirm at the sight of blood.

He nodded with a sad chuckle. "I'm glad you're here now, at any rate. We shall run the town like we always do."

Preston pursed his lips. "I can't say I've ventured out much—"

"Nonsense." Thomas crossed his arms in a likely show of seniority. At twenty-two years old, Preston was younger than his friend by two years. "I've been invited to several dinner parties already. Your invitation is secured. And there's a ball at the end of the fortnight."

Preston groaned. "I don't exactly enjoy going out like I once did."

But Thomas wouldn't hear him. "Everyone will be there. It'll be just like old times. All the ladies will wish for your conversation. You didn't lose your wit in that fire, did you?"

Preston forced a smile. He'd lost everything in that fire. Though he was glad to see Thomas's usual enthusiasm returning, he couldn't bring himself to agree with any of those plans. He wasn't the same person he had been years ago, running from party to party with his friends. Flirting and dancing the night away. He'd once had dreams, but those dreams had turned into literal nightmares. The fire had burned away every last drop of playfulness within him. He hated to crush his friend's hopes, but what choice did he have?

"Caroline!" Mother said, and Preston's stomach sank. He watched from the corner of his eye as a petite figure in blue moved down the stairs and onto the drive.

He lifted his head. Caroline Avery stood a few feet away embracing his mother. Preston's breath hitched at the very sight of her. She was dressed in a wispy blue gown, her dark blonde hair pulled back from her fair neck in a curly bun. Preston's fingers twitched remembering how soft her hand had felt in the previous summer.

"My heavens, aren't you stunning?" Mother said, and Caroline smiled widely. "How was your first ball, dear? We were so sad to miss it. You must be the talk of Society these past few months."

"Thank you, Mrs. Blake." Caroline's voice was soft as velvet, laced with the littlest of laughs. "I am quite content right here at Mayberry Park." Her eyes flickered to Preston and sobered.

How had he gone a year without seeing her face? How had he forgotten the shade of her golden hair?

"Excuse me," she said to Mother as she curtseyed.

She was walking right toward him, staring openly at his face, a question brewing in her eyes. In a moment she would see him clearly—all the ugliness that had changed him—and just like everyone else, she too would look away. She would understand why he had to send that blasted letter. Why he'd crushed every thought of a future between them.

Why had he come to Mayberry Park? If he could only turn back time, he'd stay away from the Averys for the rest of his life before having to experience this moment.

She was but feet in front of him when she stopped. Preston couldn't help it. He ducked his chin and turned his left side away from her.

"Mr. Blake," Caroline said expectantly. She wouldn't even address him by his Christian name.

Blast it all. Was he really such a coward as this? His cheeks were ablaze, his palms damp.

Preston lifted his chin slowly but fully, meeting Caroline's eyes. Her delicate blonde eyebrows were furrowed, her eyes pained as she examined him, leaning ever so slightly for a better view. Her gaze dropped to his left shoulder. Someone must have told her how the burn licked over his left side.

"Miss Avery." He bowed, hoping Thomas would intervene and save him from this humiliation.

Caroline's lips were pursed, and though he wanted to deny it, Preston would've given a hundred pounds for her thoughts.

"In your letter you spoke of extensive, unrepairable damage," Caroline's voice was demure, her eyes searching.

"I—" Preston stumbled on his words, and Caroline stared back at him, waiting without the slightest bit of the disgust he'd anticipated on her face. In fact, if he had to guess, he'd almost think she was . . . angry.

"Caroline!" Thomas whispered, his tone fierce.

"What?" Her nostrils flared like they always did when she was less than pleased, confirming Preston's guess. "He refused to let me visit based on the assumption that I was too fragile. I did not even get a chance to plead my case. My letters were not returned." Her eyes flicked to him with a look of evident pain. "I expected him to be unrecognizable."

Preston didn't know whether to find comfort in Caroline's assessment or not. His body was scarred, but so was his mind, his heart, his very soul. Given time, she might yet find him unrecognizable indeed.

Thomas looked to their parents, who conversed as though nothing was amiss between the three friends, and swallowed. "You are too blunt, Caroline. Go back into the house."

"I will not."

Preston nearly laughed aloud at her forwardness but stopped himself. Caroline deserved to be taken seriously. That same fire that forced her to speak her mind in every conversation still fumed, and he loved her all the more for it. But he did not like opposition between his friends, especially for his sake. Furthermore, he deserved her rebuke. The refusals, the letter, the silence. He'd done everything she said.

Thomas stood taller. "Then do go and join Mama. I will not allow you to slander Preston any further. He's owed you nothing this past year."

Preston flinched. He'd owed her a great deal, actually. A lifetime, in fact. Before the accident.

Whatever anger she harbored fleeted from her countenance, leaving what Preston could only imagine was a similar exhaustion and pain to his own.

"I am truly sorry if I was ever a burden," she said to him. "Or if I asked too much of you this past year. I only wanted to help. To read to you or talk to you. Anything."

Caroline paused, looking down. "I see now that we wanted very different things from each other."

Before Preston found words to respond, she swept away back toward the house. He let out a heavy breath and rubbed his jaw. Things wouldn't be the same, he'd known that. But watching her walk away from him was different than merely sending a letter.

"Preston, I must beg your pardon for Caroline's behavior. This whole year she's been rather intolerable. But especially after that ball of hers. She'd harbored some hope you'd come, I suppose. It's not as though she hasn't any callers, being newly out in Society. I don't believe it's personal." Thomas frowned, nodding toward Caroline.

Preston allowed himself another glance. He couldn't help it. The sight of Caroline dressed so properly brought a smile to his face. But despite her new elegance, she was still the same girl who pushed him into the pond fully dressed when they were children. True, it was he who had tugged the pins out of her hair just to aggravate her. But he'd liked seeing her hair flow in the wind.

Thomas continued, "She did worry after you. Hearing of your accident set her in quite a state. Your mother wrote to us and told us you were well, and we hoped you'd visit. But when you did not accept any of our invitations, especially the one to her first ball . . ."

"I have offended her." Preston said more for Thomas's sake than his own, for Thomas clearly did not know that Preston had done far worse than miss her first dance. He'd been counting the days until Caroline turned eighteen and entered Society. He'd had every intention of stealing her away after a long evening of dancing and speaking those words he'd kept locked inside his heart for so many years. He knew she felt it too. She'd nearly said so a dozen times when they were off alone together on some adventure each summer.

And when he'd held her hand last year . . . it was different than how they'd tugged each other along in younger years. Holding Caceroline's hand under the setting sun that day, he'd promised her that after their first dance together, they'd never have to part again.

He would never ask her to look at him the same way now. He was broken and scarred in the ugliest of ways, his appearance only the half of it. With all the despair and shadows in his head, the horrors he relived in his nightmares, even sometimes the paralyzing visions by day . . . how could he be happy, let alone be responsible for the happiness of another?

No, Caroline deserved far better than what he could now offer. That was why the letter had to be written. Why he had to break his promises. And his own heart in the process.

"Dinner is in an hour," Mrs. Avery said as she and her husband led Preston's mother toward the house.

Thomas patted Preston gently on the shoulder as though any pressure might further break him. "Come, let's get you settled."

∽

"WHAT DO you mean you're ill? You look perfectly fine." Mama's voice was skeptical, her eyes squinted as she peered down at Caroline laying on her bed.

"I am unwell, and I wish to take a tray in my room

tonight." Caroline leaned deeper into her pillows. She wasn't exactly sick, but her legs were weak and her throat was thick and at any moment the emotion she'd been burying so deeply in her chest might burst through its barriers. All this for a man who clearly wanted nothing to do with her.

"But you are fully dressed. You were perfectly fine a moment ago. What is this about, Caroline? Tell me at once."

"Why does it matter, Mama? The Blakes refused three of our invitations. I can certainly be absent from one dinner over the fortnight we shall have their company."

Mama clucked her teeth. "Is this because of Preston? Darling, I know you care for him. His face might take some getting used to, but we must be supportive—"

Caroline furrowed her brow. Did Mama honestly think her that shallow? "His *face* is not the change that pains me."

Caroline regretted speaking as soon as the words left her lips. Mama swooped in like a mother hen ready to shield her from any further harm. Had she heard the affection in Caroline's voice?

"Preston has endured much this past year." Mama's countenance softened as she rubbed Caroline's arm. "You must allow him a chance to redeem himself. How do you think he will feel if you do not come down?"

Caroline scooted back farther on her bed, away from Mama's reaching arms. "I am sure he won't feel anything at all anymore," she muttered.

"You do not mean that." Mama shook her head, retracting her arms. A moment passed between them, and Caroline thought back to what she'd said to Preston upon her arrival, how she'd chided him. She hadn't meant to be cold or callous. But she'd hurt enormously in his absence. Seeing him again had reminded her of all the nights she'd held onto their promises.

"Anger is often a mask for pain," Mama said as though she could see right through her. Caroline bit the inside of her bottom lip. "I have found that forgiveness—whether warranted or not—can be quite liberating."

Caroline sniffed, and looked away. Mama had no idea. She could not know of Preston's near declaration. That the change in him she most resented was not his face, but his heart. Forgiving a man for a change in affection was not like forgiving a friend over a missed appointment. Could it even be done?

Mama folded her hands together, sitting up straighter. "Very well then. I will allow you to take a tray in your room this evening."

"Oh, thank you, Mama."

"But . . ." she continued.

Caroline held her breath, bracing herself for whatever stipulation came next.

Mama stood. "I expect you awake and at your leisure for breakfast in the morning. I will not have you hiding away in your room forever. Becoming a proper lady means showing decorum despite hurt feelings. The Blakes deserve our attention, and I expect you to host them with grace and compassion."

"Yes, Mama." Caroline supposed that was fair. She'd been out in Society for three months now and had experience conversing in uncomfortable situations. She could smile and play hostess for a few hours every day. Her heart already ached, anyway. And Thomas would have activities to distract Preston, she was certain.

Mama left for dinner, leaving Caroline in the care of her maid, Martha, and alone with her thoughts. Seeing Preston after a full year had sent her heart flying like a racehorse. Caging it again had almost been more painful than the initial break after she received his letter breaking off any thought of their future together. He wouldn't make it to the party, he'd told her, and he was afraid their dance would never come. For the accident had scarred him, and he could no longer keep the promises he'd once made.

Mama had wrestled with the idea of letting Caroline write to Preston, but ultimately did not stop her. So Caroline wrote him a half a dozen letters in response. Each pleading for him to let her visit, to give her a chance to show him how little his scars would affect her, and how dearly she wanted to heal his heart. Her last letter was sent only a month before her party extending a final invitation, a last cry for reconsideration.

She heard nothing in return. Up until the very day she'd thought of Preston in every detail, and still, he hadn't come.

A small bit of her held onto hope with this visit, but Preston had hardly said a word when he saw her. Hardly fashioned a glance, and she'd put on her favorite dress. She was a proper lady now. Did he not care at all?

Had he never loved her like Caroline loved him?

If his affection had changed, then it was time she did the same. She only needed somewhere for her attention to go. There was Mr. Valcourt to distract her, she supposed, but he was more of a flattering friend and due

A BEAUTIFUL LOVE

to return to London soon. She needed someone she *truly* cared for. Someone who needed her just as much.

Romeo.

Caroline looked over her shoulder at her maid. "Have you heard any news from Hubert about Romeo, Marty?"

"Oh, yes, miss. Mr. Hubert wished me to tell you that Romeo is faring well," Marty said with an encouraging smile as she finished unpinning Caroline's gown. "If by tomorrow his limp has improved, he'll have earned his release, I'd wager."

"Already?" Caroline had found her duckling friend mauled and barely alive only three days ago and was none too eager to offer him up on a platter until he was ready to defend himself. Whatever had found him so tasty would be back to finish its meal. She'd kept a wary eye on the little one since it was a hatchling. The smallest of the bunch, he always lagged behind, and Caroline feared his slow nature would be his undoing. "I shall have to speak to Mr. Hubert first thing in the morning. Romeo was badly wounded. We cannot allow him back out until his strength has fully returned."

Marty opened her mouth as though to speak before clearing her throat and nodding. If she had an opinion, she knew better than to offer it. "As you wish, Miss Avery."

CHAPTER 2

*P*reston awoke early the next morning to an ache in his shoulder. His body was sore, likely from traveling so much yesterday. Exercise was vital in rehabilitating the strength and stretch he'd lost after his burns, or so his doctor had instructed. He'd have to stay moving today.

"Breakfast is available, should you desire it this early," his man said from the doorway.

"Thank you, Winston." Preston checked his reflection in the mirror for the tenth time. Though smooth from his nightly application of Galen's wax, his scars were ever as prominent, and he couldn't help but wonder if Caroline's sudden headache last night had been caused by the mere sight of him. Was she already making excuses to avoid him? He'd eat quickly then, and find some sort of distraction out of doors before anyone else awoke.

After descending the stairs, he slowed his steps when he heard voices coming from the direction of the breakfast room. Female voices. His heart flew up into his throat. Life was so much more comfortable at home where the only people he interacted with were Mother and his servants.

Caroline and Mrs. Avery were blocking the door to the breakfast room. Caroline's back angled toward Preston, her hands raised up in protest of whatever her mother was saying to her. Not wanting to eavesdrop, Preston took a few hesitant steps backward. Perhaps if he waited a moment, they'd walk on.

"I shall be back before anyone else comes down. Please, Mama. The matter is urgent." Caroline's voice carried down the hall.

Mrs. Avery's shoulders sank. "I will not argue with you, Caroline. You may leave the house after you break your fast with our guests. That is final."

"Nonsense. I am certain Preston does not care one bit if I am here for breakfast."

Preston snapped to attention at the mention of his name in Caroline's voice. He most certainly *did* care. Was their conversation about him?

Mrs. Avery continued, "Regardless of how Preston feels, Mrs. Blake has missed you dearly, and you are—"

"A lady now. Yes, I know." Caroline's words sounded as distasteful as sour milk.

Preston's lips twitched hearing that Caroline wasn't exactly pleased with her new role. She still knew her own mind. And like before, she was displeased with the limitations of her status. An old familiar desire to free her from the bounds of her circumstances gnawed at him. To take her away to his estate and let her wander as far as her heart desired on her own. But now his house was a hiding place—a refuge from a world that no longer belonged to him.

No matter how impossible his long held dreams seemed, the piece inside him that wanted to save Caroline hated to see her upset and confined. Perhaps he could guide her mother into agreement, as he had so many times before, and at least grant Caroline a morning of freedom. Seeing her happy would be worth a stare or two. He stepped into their view.

"Good morning, Mrs. Avery. Miss Avery."

Caroline turned toward him, wide-eyed.

"Mr. Blake." Mrs. Avery curtseyed with a smile. "You've just arrived in time to join Caroline and me to break our fasts."

Caroline let out a wary breath through her nose, looking sullenly at the ceiling.

"Perhaps I will find you when I've returned from my morning walk, if you don't mind." Preston overindulged his shoulders in a healthy stretch. "Unless . . ." He hesitated, suddenly doubting his plan. If things went as bluntly as they had yesterday, she'd surely reject his offer and leave him feeling ridiculous for thinking them friends. "Would you care to join me, Miss Avery?"

Her eyes flicked up at him, and Preston turned to Mrs. Avery. "With your permission, of course."

Mrs. Avery glanced suspiciously between them. They'd been known to scheme together in the past. To hide away in the fields with Thomas until dinner. But things were clearly different now. The offer was innocent enough.

Caroline nodded, and Preston cursed his happy heart.

"A *quick* walk. And do stay close to the house. I will be

in the breakfast room when you return." Mrs. Avery looked unimpressed and narrowed her eyes at her daughter as she passed into the room. If she knew Preston had meddled, she must not have minded too terribly.

The obvious detail Preston hadn't fully considered in his haste to save Caroline from her mother was that he'd actually have to escort her on a walk. Alone.

Preston's mind went blank, and the hallway turned hot. He'd let his heart get away with him again and hadn't thought his offer through rationally. This was exactly what he'd been trying to avoid. Things couldn't go back to the way they were. Trying would lead to failure and failure would only break him more.

Standing face to face, Preston scratched the back of his neck, thinking wildly for something, anything to say. Caroline studied his face and surely his scars, and Preston cleared his throat. He knew she was only curious, but something inside him sunk when she examined his new ugliness. Better to just start moving. "Shall we?" he asked her, motioning down the hall.

Slowly, Caroline nodded her head again and turned on a heel. The hallway quaked with silence as Preston followed Caroline toward the entry. Three steps around the corner and they were out the door, greeted by morning sunlight. Caroline was a few paces ahead of Preston, and he chided himself inwardly for not offering her his arm. That would have been the polite thing to do, even if they could only ever be friends. If nothing else, doing so might have slowed her down. Preston was practically at a run to keep up with her increasingly hasty pace.

"Where exactly are we going?" he asked when he reached her.

She shot him a sideways glance. "To the stablehouse."

The stablehouse? Caroline was not an avid rider. Unless her interests had changed in the past year. He sighed. As she walked beside him, her shoulders were stiff and her chin raised. There was no laughter or teasing, and the space between them spanned closer to two feet than one. Couldn't they still be friends? Friends still joked and shared secrets and spent time together. He could at least try.

"Might I ask what draws you there?" he asked.

Caroline didn't waste a moment. She turned on him as quickly as a frog to a fly. "Might I ask what compelled you to miss my party? You did not even send word back."

Preston's tongue went dry. He nearly tripped on a clump of dirt in the pathway.

Caroline was relentless. He'd thought it obvious enough, must he say it aloud? Had he gone to the ball, everyone would have stared and grimaced at his appearance. They would have pitied Caroline, or worse, assumed she felt an obligation to her childhood friend. Not to mention the gossip, the rumors that would have followed. Surely she was not so naive as she pretended to be.

"Perhaps the same reason you decided to take dinner in your room last night." A headache was too easy an excuse.

"That I doubt very much." Caroline's tone had gone soft, somber even. She looked ahead to the stablehouse that grew nearer with each step. Preston could already smell the scent of fresh hay and oats from the horses' breakfast.

He exhaled, hating to argue. He wished things between them could go back to the way they were last summer. But time could not be turned back. Even if it could, he'd do the same thing over again. He'd still run into that burning house to save his tenants, even knowing the losses he would endure.

"You have not changed one bit, Caroline," Preston said in half-annoyance, half-affection.

She stopped just outside the door leading in to the stalls. "That I have not. Have you?"

Preston's brow furrowed. He was obviously changed and growing tired of Caroline's inability to accept it. "You need not pretend you are blind. It is obvious I am not the same man I was a year ago."

Caroline squinted, shaking her head at him. "Heavens, if anyone is blind between us, it is you."

She turned and pushed through the stablehouse door, leaving Preston in her wake, confused and unsettled. Why did women speak in riddles? He hadn't been out much this past year, it was true, but he'd never been *that* terrible at deciphering social cues. He caught the door with a hand and followed her inside.

"His name is Romeo," Caroline said over her shoulder as she unlatched a stall. Preston peeked over her head. It was empty, save for a large crate in the back corner.

Where was the horse? Had Caroline gone mad? Or was he truly blind?

"I found him a few days ago by the pond badly wounded and carried him here. Mr. Hubert helped me nurse him back to health." Caroline's whole demeanor had lifted. "Romeo!"

A blanket in the corner shifted, and Preston took a step back. What the devil had he gotten himself into?

Caroline lifted the blanket and out popped a tiny beaked head. A duckling.

"Miss Avery," Mr. Hubert approached the gate, coming face to face with Preston. The man jumped back. "Ah, uh—and Mr. Blake, sir." Immediately Mr. Hubert looked down, and Preston winced. The Averys' groom had known him for years. It was fair for him to react to Preston's face. Everyone was entitled to that first moment of shock.

"He is looking well, Mr. Hubert," Caroline said, oblivious to the reaction. "But I fear his leg is not quite healed."

Upon closer observation, the duckling was hardly a duckling at all in size. Looking more like a winged rat, it was badly mauled with patches of red, ugly skin showing all over its body. "What happened to it?" he asked as Caroline brought the creature to him.

"We're not sure," Caroline answered. "Lucifer usually scares off most predators around the pond. Something small must have slipped through."

"Lucifer is still alive, then." Preston couldn't help but smile. That old goose was a legend. As children, Preston and Thomas would dare each other to provoke him. Bloody ankles usually resulted, but once, Lucifer got the better of Thomas, and Preston had to fight the goose off with a stick. Neither boy was quick to return to the pond after that.

"A few more days of recovery," Caroline said to Mr. Hubert. "I truly believe he needs it."

"What he needs is to return to his family, miss," Mr. Hubert argued kindly. "I've little time to keep an eye on him. Staying in this stall is doing him a disservice. He needs to be among his own kind and learn to feed himself."

Caroline let the little duck down in the crate, and it waddled back to the blanket. Preston noticed a small bowl of water and food as well. Mr. Hubert was right. They weren't doing the thing any favors by coddling it.

"Three more days. I shall deliver him to the pond myself." Caroline's shoulders fell, and Preston felt that familiar pull to rescue her from any sadness. Try as he might to suppress it, wanting to protect Caroline came as naturally to Preston as breathing.

"I will make sure of it, Mr. Hubert," he offered.

Caroline raised a brow at him as though to say, '*Will you, now?*' and walked back over to the corner of the stall to say a last goodbye.

Preston let out a weary breath and turned to Mr. Hubert. "Do you have any guess as to what attacked him?"

The man lowered his voice. "Honestly, I've no idea. But Miss Caroline was awful upset by it. The gamekeeper scouted around but found no tracks. We are continuing the search at Miss Avery's request. I've known the girl since she was born, and she's attached herself to this lot. Seeing her heartache is unbearable. I'd hate for whatever it was to come back and finish the job. But what can I do? A duck don't belong in a horse's stable, Mr. Blake."

"Indeed," Preston agreed. He watched as Caroline

kissed the duck on the head and allowed himself a sad smile. To be so lucky.

"I must attend breakfast, but I will be back to see Romeo this afternoon," she said to Mr. Hubert.

"As you wish, Miss Avery." He bowed.

Caroline turned to make her exit, not sparing him a second glance. Preston looked heavenward for support. Never had they been so indifferent to one another.

This time, Preston would not be so daft and fail to offer his arm. Seeing Caroline care for her duck reminded him of how much he'd missed her. There was so much to admire in her. Her gentleness, her compassion, her patience. How she'd barely flinched when she saw his face yesterday.

His wounds ran much deeper than scarring, though. She could heal a duck, but she could never fix Preston's mind, his memories. If he wanted to be a part of her life, even just to renew their friendship, he needed to make things right while he was here.

Offering his arm, he said, "Shall we return together, Car—" Preston stopped himself. He wanted their easy familiarity back, but did she feel the same?

He cleared his throat. "Miss Avery?"

Whether she did not see him, or she purposefully ignored his arm, Preston didn't know for sure. Caroline's gaze was focused downward as her feet carried her through the stablehouse doors.

~

KEEP YOURSELF TOGETHER, Caroline told herself, maintaining her focus as she walked.

"You must be hungry, walking in such haste," he said with obvious levity.

"This is a normal pace, Preston. For those of us who leave our houses on a regular basis." The words left her before she could retract them, and she tightened her lips together at once. This wasn't like her, angry and bitter and cruel. But *he* had chosen not to come to her ball, not to dance with her like he'd promised. He was the one who called everything off. And he'd locked himself away for so long without speaking a word. He was her closest friend, or had been, at least. How else would he know how badly he'd hurt her with his absence unless she told him?

Preston bowed his head and her heart sank. He knew. He had to know.

"Preston, I—" She started to apologize, but Preston cut her off.

"I'll have you know I get out of doors plenty. If not more so than before. I've improved my estate tenfold since you last visited." A hint of pride touched Preston's voice. Then he gave her a chuckle. "As for my pace, I have never felt so strong. I could easily lift a dozen of you."

Caroline whipped her head around in astonishment. Preston was joking with her. Just like in boyhood when he'd try to impress her by throwing logs into the pond. "You are despicable," she said, unable to contain her grin.

Preston smiled back unashamed. "I've always been despicable. But you . . . you have never been mean."

Caroline felt a quake in her chest, a softening perhaps. She'd wanted a reaction from Preston, and here it was. They were midway to the house, both slowing. The morning sun grew warm upon their backs.

"I must beg your forgiveness," he continued softly, more seriously. "For making promises I could not keep."

She knew he spoke of that sunset a year ago, when he'd held her hand and promised to escort her, to stand with her for the first set at her own party. To never leave her again. She'd thought his feelings matched her own. She'd thought their dance would be the first of many. The first of a new beginning between them. She'd hoped Preston would finally admit his feelings that night. He *had* to have felt what she did that summer. Why did he abandon her? What, beyond scars on the side of his face, had changed?

"That is precisely the thing, Preston. You could have kept your promises. But you chose not to." Pain threatened to surface, pricking at the corners of Caroline's eyes like dew on the grass. She sniffed and turned from him, continuing her walk to the house.

This time, Preston kept pace.

"I wanted to, but—"

"We needn't do this." Caroline's voice came out passive, meek, though she felt shaken to the core. She wanted him to speak, but at the same time could hardly bear his excuse. He didn't love her. Not like she'd hoped. Hearing him voice his indifference would only cause her further pain.

"If there is anything I can do . . . or anything I can say to earn your forgiveness," Preston's hand gently tugged at Caroline's arm. "You need only say the word. I'll oblige you this minute if it means we can be friends again."

Stopping, she turned to face him. His warm chocolate eyes were light and clear in the sunlight. The same as they'd always been. Looking at her the same way they always had. He wanted her friendship. Why now? After a full year away.

"Where have you been?" She swallowed, looking anywhere but into those kind brown eyes. She wanted to trust him, but even allowing him friendship meant opening her heart to him. "Your mother said you've been well for months. Why did you not accept any of our invitations? Why did you keep me away all this time?"

His feet shuffled, driving thick footprints into the soft earth. "I do not socialize much anymore," Preston said as though he'd rehearsed the answer. "And you're the very center of attention now, I am sure."

She nodded. Preston's life had changed drastically to be sure. He used to love going to dinner parties and balls with Thomas, and still he'd chosen a future with Caroline. Didn't he know that despite the accident she would never have abandoned him? Indeed, she'd do anything to help him even now.

"I truly want your friendship, Caroline. I hate knowing you are angry with me. And I can't bear knowing that I've hurt you." Preston's eyes filled with concern, and even though Caroline's heart felt close to breaking all over again, she wanted his friendship, too. Desperately.

"I want that, too. Truly, I hate that you've suffered so much on your own, Preston. But I shall try to understand your decisions." She stared seriously into his gaze. "For now, no more making promises you cannot keep. If we are to be friends, I want the honesty of our childhood back. Like when you'd tell me my hair smelled like a horse or that Cook had fed me too well that year."

Preston's lips twitched into a laugh. "I really am despicable."

"I am in earnest, Preston." Caroline crossed her arms, determined to be heard. "One thing I have learned from being out in Society is that integrity and trust are hard to come by. I am tired of deciphering a person's thoughts or intentions based on snippets of clues they give in conversation. I don't wish to guess with you."

Preston's smile grew warm, like he was seeing her fully again, and he bit his lip for a moment. "I suppose I can agree to that. As long as you promise to try and view things from my perspective. My version of honesty might not be as agreeable to you as it once was."

Caroline wasn't quite sure what Preston meant by that, but surely she could step into his shoes when necessary. "Very well, then. Friends."

"Wonderful." Preston held out his hand with that same grin widening upon his face.

Caroline hesitated for just a moment. Could she trust Preston with a bit of her heart? She looked into his eyes and found only familiar kindness there. There was no bitterness or distaste or pity, nor any reason for her to believe he disliked her or that his opinion of her had lessened. Indeed, whatever passed between them in that moment begged Caroline's heart to wonder if things between them had changed at all in the past year.

No, it wouldn't do to allow such fantasy anymore. Here was reality right in front of her. She should count herself lucky to have her friend back, even if their pact was made out of convenience because Preston would be sharing her home for the fortnight. This was better than tiptoeing around the estate.

She extended her hand, and Preston gave it a gentle squeeze before tucking her arm in his. Warmth spread like honey all the way down to her toes.

"Shall we continue to breakfast?" he asked.

Caroline nodded and a smile of her own broke through at Preston's warmth and nearness. "I am famished."

"I knew it," Preston said triumphantly. "I know you so well."

"And yet we've much to discuss after a year apart."

They'd arrive back in minutes, but Caroline still had so much she wanted to say. To ask. An entire year had passed, leaving Caroline with a mind full of unanswered questions. She barely knew the details of the fire, let alone how Preston recovered from it.

Preston must've sensed her curiosity. His eyes met hers in an almost helpless, wounded sort of way. Was a year too soon to speak of such things? They used to talk about everything.

The house was mere feet away, and Preston slowed his steps as though they had all the time in the world. "You first, then. Who took my place at your party?"

Caroline moaned internally. Must they start with that night? "Mr. Edwin Valcourt of London."

"Do I know him?" Preston furrowed an eyebrow.

"I doubt it. Though you likely will." Something inside Caroline stirred. Was Preston curious about her suitor? She hadn't taken Mr. Valcourt too seriously, but with no other man in her future, she wondered if she ought to be more considerate of the matter. Or at least gauge Preston's reaction. She raised her chin and continued, "He's in line for an earldom. Very handsome, very wealthy. Everything my mother wishes for in a match."

"I see." Preston stared ahead to the house. "And has he called on you often?"

"Quite often, actually." Caroline bit her lip, watching him. "Father thinks he will offer for me before he returns to London in a few weeks. I cannot imagine it is all that serious, though."

Preston drew in a breath and let out a huff of air. "Interesting."

"As my friend, you shall have to give me your opinion of him." Caroline said. Preston was stoic. He walked with her on his right side, and she wondered if he faced her that way on purpose.

"Shall I?" His words were clipped, unenthusiastic. "What does Thomas say?"

"They get on, though Thomas has been distracted himself of late. By a Miss Talent," Caroline said airily. "It is as though his world has stopped."

Preston was quiet, seemingly lost in thought as he held the door open for her. "Well, I am happy for you, then. The both of you."

Caroline blinked. That was it? Had they not promised only moments ago to be honest with one another?

He must truly not feel what I feel. Caroline passed through the door, her heart in her throat. It wouldn't do to cry at breakfast. She'd already shed enough tears for Preston Blake.

An instant waft of eggs and apple pastry distracted Caroline, and she headed straight for the spread. Apples were in season, and she rather loved Cook's apple cinnamon pastries. A half dozen would satisfy her this morning. And if she felt uneasy still, she'd fill her plate again. As much as she wanted friendship with Preston, she hardly knew how to keep her feelings locked away. But as usual, she had little say in the matter. The choice was his, not hers.

CHAPTER 3

*T*wo days had already passed at Mayberry Park before Mr. Edwin Valcourt came to call. Mother stole Preston from his room, where he'd just finished correspondence to his steward back home.

Why Mother thought Preston needed to make the man's acquaintance was beyond him, but he had promised Caroline his opinion, and he had no desire to break another promise to her.

The first thing he noticed upon entering the drawing room was Valcourt's hair. It was piled atop his head like a billowing cloud making him half a foot taller than he actually was. His cravat was tied three times over, and his boots shined as though he'd never stepped foot out of doors.

"Mr. Blake." Mr. Avery ushered Preston inside. Mrs. Avery, Caroline, and Mother formed a half circle around Valcourt. "Allow me to introduce Mr. Edwin Valcourt, a new friend of the family."

"A pleasure," Mr. Valcourt said brusquely. He spared

no reserve in openly staring, clearly displaying his distaste for Preston's appearance and barely bowing.

"Likewise." Preston returned a half-hearted bow. He looked to Caroline and found her studying his reaction.

He couldn't decide if he was more annoyed by the dandy's tastes or blatant rudeness. Was Caroline truly interested in *this* man?

A rat had better manners.

"It is too bad we cannot join you as a group. Had we only organized better," Mrs. Avery said to Valcourt, who offered a sly smile.

"Indeed, it must have slipped my mind that you were hosting company this week. But surely we will have more time together. I promise to return Miss Avery to you after the picnic in good health. My grandmama eagerly awaits her company in our carriage." Valcourt held his smile too perfectly in place and offered his arm to Caroline, who moved to accept it.

How could he have forgotten such a big event in Caroline's schedule? Clearly, this man was weaseling his way into the Averys' good opinion and using every angle to his advantage. Everyone knew the Averys were a wealthy family. And Caroline was . . . well, a beauty to say the least. But Caroline still seemed so inexperienced and naive. Someone needed to keep a close eye on her and an even closer eye on Valcourt. Perhaps that someone ought to be her brother.

Preston's eyes darted around the room. Where on earth *was* Thomas? The man had been out nearly every afternoon. Preston had only seen his friend in the mornings when the two would venture off on estate errands together.

Before another word was uttered, Valcourt slithered his way to the door with Caroline, and Preston watched through slatted eyes from the middle of the room.

"He seems quite a catch," Mother said, raising a brow to him.

Preston shook his head. Normally when Society stared at him, he cringed or looked away. But there was something deeper in Valcourt's stare. Some condescending, hateful thought behind those eyes that made Preston want to call him out on the spot. "You cannot be serious. Did you see the way he stared at me? The man is a fop."

"Oh come, Preston. As you've said a thousand times, everyone stares at you. Besides, I see no one else here to claim Caroline's afternoon. Mr. Valcourt deserves a chance."

Preston couldn't believe his ears, nor the happy smile upon Mother's lips. Her eyes practically sparkled as she turned to follow the Averys out of the drawing room. She had to be toying with him. What did everyone see in Valcourt?

"Luncheon is served," a servant called a few minutes later. That, at least, would offer a good enough distraction for now.

Even better, Thomas finally joined them just as they'd all settled in. His hair was sleek and his usual attire more fashionable and crisp. Wherever had he been? Or where was he going?

When their plates were cleared and conversation lulled into satisfied drowsiness, Thomas leaned toward Preston.

"Care to join me for a ride?" he asked under his breath. "I need a favor, if you don't mind."

"Anything," Preston answered quickly, throwing his napkin onto the table and straightening his coat. Anything to pass the time.

Besides, this would be a perfect opportunity to confront Thomas about Valcourt.

Clouds were beginning to fill the sky when they finally stepped out of doors. Perhaps it would rain, and Caroline would be forced home early from her picnic. Preston felt unsettled the longer she spent with Valcourt. Where had they gone exactly? Did the two of them even have any common interests? And was Valcourt's grandmama an attentive enough chaperone? Preston drew a heavy breath, trying to calm the nerves that rose to his chest. He didn't relish the idea of Caroline having suitors, but since he couldn't be the one to stand beside her, he wanted to be sure the man she chose was worthy of the position.

"I hate to use you like this. But I knew you wouldn't mind," Thomas was saying when Preston turned his attention back to him.

Preston raised a brow at his friend.

"My parents forbade me from calling on her while you both are here." Thomas shook his head. "But I cannot go without seeing Julia. You understand, don't you?"

Preston looked up in alarm. "We're going to meet your Miss Talent?" He'd only just settled in with the Averys. Must he endure more uncomfortable introductions already?

"I happen to know she rides every afternoon to the top of the hill." A smile curled Thomas's lips. "I've had to sneak around to catch her, but I'm afraid Mama is growing suspicious."

Preston shouldn't feel discouraged, especially when Thomas's eyes were as lit with excitement as they were. Was it selfish to wish for time alone with his friend? At least they weren't going into town. If they wanted to keep Mrs. Avery from suspicion, this would likely be a quick ride. A moment for Thomas to fill his heart and then the two of them could have their time. Pushing his own thoughts aside, Preston feigned an encouraging grin and said, "Then up the hill we shall go."

Thomas had been in such a rush, neither had said more than two words to the other before they reached the stables. "We must be quick to not miss her," Thomas added, leading his horse to the yard.

Preston mounted, and Thomas waited only a moment before coaxing his steed into a full run. The wind passed over Preston's face and through his jacket as they raced through the pasture. A shortcut, it seemed. Preston's steed was happy with the exercise, easily keeping pace with Thomas. Unfortunately, such speed allowed for little to no conversation.

When they reached the hill, there was already someone there waiting for them. A few someones, actually. Indeed, as they rode to the top, a group awaited them.

Preston's throat grew thick, his palms sweaty. Three ladies and two gentlemen, with a few servants as well. Thomas greeted a small woman dressed in a red riding habit, leaving Preston at the edge of the party alone. He could feel stolen glances upon him as he awaited an introduction but stared ahead at the woody scene on the other side of the hill. He'd have to make an excuse to exit as quickly as possible.

"Mr. Preston Blake."

Looking up, all five faces were examining his, each with varying degrees of pity and distaste. The left side of his face tingled, and he squirmed like a mouse under the claws of a cat. His cravat covered the welting skin at his neck, but not enough of his jaw, nor the lapping from fire that had burned up his cheek toward the side of his nose.

"A pleasure," Preston said, nodding his head. One young lady in particular raised her chin and frowned.

"Remind me not to challenge Mr. Blake to a duel," a gentleman said, nodding to Preston's face. He was grinning through his arrogance, like he was the bravest among them for being willing to mention the scars.

Thomas shot the man a disapproving scowl, and Preston took a shallow breath.

"A fire," he said dully, lifting his hand to acknowledge the left side of his face. Neither this man, nor any in his company deserved the full story.

"You're right lucky to be alive judging by those scars," another man said.

Preston adjusted his riding gloves. They had no idea, the lot of them. And he had no time nor patience to endure the questioning of strangers and wait for them to become comfortable with his face.

"I am, though I pay for it every day. If you'll excuse me. I must cut my ride short, as I have business to attend to this afternoon. Good day." Preston nodded to Thomas, who looked ready to protest, but it was Miss Talent who broke away from the group.

"Mr. Blake." She looked to Preston and smiled

sweetly. Deep brown curls framed her porcelain face. "I am so happy to meet you. I hope you'll forgive my brothers their forwardness. I fear we are too familiar, with you knowing so little of us. Thomas speaks often of you and the adventures of your childhood."

Preston gave her a small bow of his head. She was kind to say as much, true or not. "I hope you enjoy his company as much I as do. He is a good man."

"I quite agree. I hope we shall see you again very soon. At a better time, perhaps." Miss Talent slackened her hold on her horse's reigns to free his head.

"Indeed." Preston smiled. Thomas had done well for himself after all.

When the hill was out of sight, Preston relaxed and pulled back on his horse. Perhaps he ought to care about leaving his friend behind, but had Thomas given him any warning about Miss Talent's party? Preston shook his head. He knew deep down none of their reactions were Thomas's fault, but his hopes for the afternoon were completely squandered. His friends, both of them, had their own lives to live.

Back at the stables, Preston's muscles groaned as he dismounted. The truth was evident. He couldn't have Caroline without disappointing her, nor could he walk alongside Thomas in Society comfortably. Because of that fire, Preston no longer belonged . . . anywhere. He had his home in Hereford, of course. And he'd always have Mother. But soon, Thomas, and perhaps even Caroline, would marry and be chained to the expectations of Society. Would this be Preston's last visit to Mayberry Park? He hadn't considered that.

After giving his horse to Mr. Hubert, Preston started

on a quick walk to stretch his legs before heading in. He rounded the front of the building and was just about to return to the house when he saw her.

Caroline was walking alone directly toward him, far enough away to be completely unaware of anyone watching her. Her arms were hanging freely by her sides. Gone was the straightened back and high held chin of who she pretended to be in her parents' presence. She looked content and happy in her solitude. Or was Valcourt the source of her renewed joy?

The thought put a dirty taste in Preston's mouth. How was it fair that a man like Valcourt could strut around however he wanted, while Preston had to mentally prepare himself for every outing? Sometimes merely getting out of bed to face the day was a challenge after reliving that tragic morning in his nightmares.

At least Caroline was his friend. He was starting to believe she didn't look at his scars like everyone else did. Indeed, she hadn't shied away from him since their morning in the stables two days ago.

Then realization struck.

Romeo. She's going to visit Romeo.

Without so much as a second thought, Preston turned back, calling out for Mr. Hubert.

~

CLOUDS OVERCASTING the sky made Romeo's stall darker than usual.

"Where are you, my little duck?" she called, lifting the blanket where he usually hid.

Empty?

Caroline's chest constricted and she spun around, searching desperately for Romeo. He was not in his stall.

"Mr. Hubert!" she called as she raced out the back door toward the pastures.

Her plea was answered with a man's chuckling.

Preston stood side by side with Mr. Hubert. Further beyond the men was Romeo, waddling around freely in the grass. Caroline raised a hand to her chest.

"Miss Avery." Preston bowed. Though his smile was genuine, there was darkness in his countenance. Sadness. "I hope you don't mind, but we thought Romeo was due to stretch his legs."

"Thank heavens. I thought somehow he'd been . . ." Caroline couldn't finish her thought.

"Eaten? Not on my watch," Preston said with confidence. His hands were on his hips as he looked on to where Romeo grazed.

A smile twitched at Caroline's lips. She knew Preston was exaggerating loyalty to Romeo, that he likely thought keeping a duck in a horse's stall was ridiculous and childish, but for some reason he cared enough to give time to the cause. He was being a good friend. Her shoulders lifted at his earnest attempt.

Judging by the somber look in his eyes, perhaps she needed to return the favor.

"Mr. Hubert, how is the search? Have you found any curious footprints or markings around the pond?" Caroline asked.

"Nothing unusual, Miss Avery. The predator, whatever it is, either lives among us or is particularly light on its feet," he responded.

Romeo waddled near Caroline, and she bent down to

examine him. Though his skin was healed, his body would need to regrow several patches of feathers, leaving too much of him exposed to the elements.

"It's been two days since we spoke last about Romeo returning to the pond. But as you can see, he is thriving." Mr. Hubert scratched his chin. "Mr. Blake's offered to assist you in returning him now. Of course, if anything were to happen—"

"Nothing will happen," Preston interjected. "Romeo here will be just fine back with his family."

Caroline rose from her spot. The yard in front of them suddenly expanded for miles. "But he has one more day."

The men exchanged a glance. "He is ready, Miss Avery," Mr. Hubert said kindly.

As though on cue, Romeo offered a small quack in what Caroline could only assume was agreeance. What could she do? Sneaking Romeo into her bedchamber would be a disaster. By no means would Martha keep the secret. She could hear Mama's voice in her head lecturing on the rightful places for ducks and the separation of proper ladies from such activities. *How will you secure a husband with a duck in your bedchamber?* she'd surely shriek. Besides, anyone with eyes could see that Romeo thrived out of doors. The little thing quacked and hobbled and munched on grass like he'd just come out of hibernation.

But he was still so small. And so fragile.

"You'll keep eyes on him? Watch for any signs of predators?" Caroline asked Mr. Hubert. "You'll check on him first thing in the morning?"

"I will," he replied, nodding firmly.

Caroline looked to Preston and found his brown eyes

searching hers. Her heart did a sudden leap at his attention, though she knew from his own words he only thought of her as a friend. Mr. Valcourt often looked at her with a similar intensity, but his searching left her uncomfortable, as opposed to the safety she felt with Preston.

"Where is his basket?" she asked, referring to the small picnic basket she'd used to carry him from the pond to the stables. That frightful afternoon seemed like just yesterday, though it was over a week ago.

"Just here." Preston procured it from a few paces away, and Mr. Hubert bowed, taking his leave of them.

Together, they made quick work of herding Romeo into Caroline's cupped hands. With the duck safely deposited into the basket, Caroline laced it onto her arm and led Preston behind the stables toward the pond. The worn dirt footpath that connected the two places provided just enough walking space for the two of them.

How many times had they made this very walk? A thousand, if Caroline had to guess. As a girl, she'd chased Thomas and Preston down the dirt path on all their adventures. As they grew older, Preston would escort her on long walks in the summer to escape the boredom of stitching or practicing the pianoforte relentlessly. And last summer they'd walked these very same steps together hand in hand, laughing about the trouble their mothers would give them if they only knew what mischief they'd caused in their youth.

Though they never spoke such things aloud, Caroline knew Preston too had wondered about their futures. Some part of him, at least for a moment, had considered a future where the two of them lived happily ever after.

Caroline could only imagine what her life might be like had Preston not run into that burning house. Not that she wished harm upon the family that had been trapped inside. She shivered at the thought and couldn't begin to imagine how it must have felt to be so helpless, so desperate.

But why was Preston the first to happen upon their house that morning? Why did their savior have to be him?

"Are you worrying after him still?" Preston's voice was low, thoughtful, and Caroline blinked away her thoughts. He nodded to Romeo, who shuffled around in the basket as they walked.

"I cannot help it," Caroline answered, tightening her grip upon the basket. She worried after the both of them, honestly.

"If you'd like, I can come back this evening with a lantern and check on him before I retire."

She looked up. "Truly?"

Preston huffed lightheartedly, as though he was appalled that she took him as anything less than sincere. "Of course. I know you well enough to know that sleep will not come easily to you tonight. And what are friends for if not to sneak out in the middle of the night and stalk poor ducks while they sleep?"

Caroline bit back a laugh. They drew nearer to the pond which was surrounded by cattle and pasture. "Thank you, then. I shall expect a full report under my door this evening."

"A secret note. That won't lead us into trouble." Preston raised a knowing brow.

"Not unless you are caught."

Preston leaned closer. "I am never caught."

That was true. Growing up, Preston had been stealth personified. He could scale a tree in twenty seconds or camouflage himself in the middle of an open field for the sake of staying out of trouble. The fact had been maddening to Caroline on most occasions.

Preston locked his hands behind his back. "How did you come to christen your duck with such a name anyway?"

Caroline grinned. "I named him Romeo because I fell in love with him the moment I saw him."

Preston looked toward the heavens with feigned exhaustion.

"And," she added on a laugh, "I quite enjoy calling out for him." Caroline cupped her hand around her mouth. "'Romeo, Romeo. Wherefore art thou, Romeo?'"

Preston chuckled. "Shakespeare would roll over in his grave to have a duck play his lead."

Caroline smiled to herself. Making Preston laugh used to come so easily. She reveled in the sound and wanted more.

Romeo grew restless in the basket as they approached the pond, the sound of distant quacking floating toward him. Setting the basket down, Caroline opened the lid and gently lifted him out and onto the grass.

Romeo was off like lightning. First, he stretched out his wings, fluttering and causing the smallest of stirs in the breeze. He let out a string of noises which were instantly returned by his siblings swimming a few yards away. Knowing his new destination, he didn't hesitate, but wobbled to the bank's edge and plopped into the water as though he'd never left.

Caroline watched the reunion fondly, but disappointment loomed. It had been nice to be needed. The routine of checking on her little friend and being so lovingly received each morning when she brought his breakfast had become her favorite part of the day. Would he not miss her as she would miss him? Would he offer her no thanks?

Of course not. He was a duck.

Preston knelt down beside Caroline. "See, there? You worry for nothing. He is back where he belongs."

Caroline glanced sideways at Preston. She hated when he was right. But at least he didn't have Thomas's echo behind him. "Where is Thomas? Mama said you were out with him."

Preston stretched out on the grass beside her, watching as the ducks swam together in circles. "Thomas and I went for a ride, but I grew tired of it early."

Of course! Thomas had broken his promise to Mama and went off to see Julia. And used Preston to keep his secrets. She should have known. "And how do you like Miss Talent?"

Preston jerked his head toward her. "I didn't say—"

"I won't tell Mama." Caroline held back a smile.

Preston relaxed on a breath. "She is kind. Refined. And Thomas seems besotted by her."

"He is. If he weren't such a ninny, he'd have already proposed."

"You like her, then?"

Caroline nodded. "She is a friend. I think they will do well together. She brings out a happier side of him."

Preston smiled to himself. "I shall have to encourage him then while I am here."

Caroline studied the side of his face left untouched by the fire. His jawline was a perfect square and smoothed from his morning shave. From this view, he looked exactly the same as he did in her memories. They sat together observing the bustling grass and wind hewn ripples on the pond. Preston's hand was inches from hers.

A loud honk sounded from behind them.

"Lucifer!" they said in tandem, standing immediately. Sure enough, that old goose with weather beaten wings and the scariest bulge on his beak was stalking toward them with purpose. That a goose could incite such terror was nonsensical, but Caroline, and she was certain Preston as well, knew the power of that bird's beak.

"Do you think he recognizes me?" Preston's eyes were lit with worry.

Caroline could see the boy in him from their childhood. She grinned, feeling just as youthful. "Of course he recognizes you. He likely revels in your old age."

Preston studied her a moment, and she nudged him playfully. Slowly, his lips broke into a grin and he took a step back. Lucifer was drawing near and lowering his awful neck. "Perhaps if I lean my left side toward him, he'll feel intimidated by my bravery and scars and change his course to attack you."

"Preston!" Caroline squealed, pointing to the goose who was now hissing only feet from them. She pounded upon his chest, the past year entirely forgotten. "Do something!"

"It's working!" He laughed, but the sound was cut short when Lucifer lunged at Caroline.

She didn't have time to scream, for Preston had her

scooped up to his chest, lifting her completely off the ground as he kicked at Lucifer's insistent biting.

"Come off it, you!" he growled, jumping away to save his ankles. "She is a lady now. Won't you show some decorum?"

Caroline laughed, holding Preston around the neck. She buried her face near his collarbone as he squirmed away from Lucifer's reach.

"Ow, gads, man!" he whined, dancing a few steps backward. Caroline looked up just as the old goose hissed one last time for good measure before hobbling back toward his perch at the edge of the pond. Preston seemed only half assured of their safety, still holding onto Caroline tightly.

"Are you all right?" As her heart calmed and her senses realigned, she became keenly aware of her position.

Preston was holding her. She was *completely* encircled by his arms.

When was the last time she felt so ... full? She leaned into him again, resting her head against his. He smelled like grass and honey. For the shortest moment, she thought she felt him lean in too.

"Yes," Preston answered, taking another full breath. "I've rather missed that goose." Gently, and all too soon, he lowered her to a standing position. Caroline noticed right away a ruddiness in his cheeks from exertion or ... embarrassment? He took a small step backward and straightened his jacket.

Caroline's legs were as wobbly as jelly.

"I nominated him for Christmas dinner last year, but Father said he would be too tough," she jested.

"Caroline Avery, my word." Preston pretended to be astounded, and they both laughed aloud.

"You'd have eaten him, too. Need I remind you of the time he ripped a hole in your breeches?"

Preston sobered. "That was humiliating. The Farthing girls were here."

"They are both married and ridiculous now, so perhaps he did you a favor."

Preston smiled and looked off toward the pond. Caroline wondered what he was thinking. He was usually so free with his mind.

"Shall we return to the house before our mothers suspect us of running away?" he asked.

"If we must," Caroline said on a sigh. Romeo still floated on the pond with his family. It was true; he belonged with them. He *fit* with his family in a way Caroline envied ardently. She loved Mama and Father, even Thomas. But she still felt as though something were missing. She wanted something of her own. A home where she fit as perfectly as Romeo fit with his.

Preston had once been that something. And when he held her in his arms, she could swear she belonged right there, forever.

How could he not feel it too?

CHAPTER 4

Stop. Thinking. Of. Caroline.

Preston repeated the phrase twenty times before getting out of bed the next morning. He'd spent a good hour late last night watching Romeo and keeping an eye out for anything threatening. And staying far away from Lucifer, of course, who slept with one leg tucked under his belly and one beady eye left open.

After scribbling a quick note, slipping it under her door, and sliding into bed, Preston had tossed and turned all evening remembering how it felt to hold Caroline in his arms. She'd leaned into him, laughed with him, wanted him.

He couldn't stop himself from wondering what their lives could be like together. Perhaps they'd be happy in the beginning, running around the estate on their usual adventures. But the time would come, he was sure of it, where Caroline would grow restless. Where she would ask for more than he could give. Whether she cared to admit it or not, like her family, she was a social creature who needed interaction with society now and again. But Preston had no desire to step out into the light. Not anymore. Not like he had in the past.

So he couldn't think of Caroline. Not if it meant wishing he could hold her again, or sneak away with her again, or steal a glance, a touch.

A kiss.

Preston wiped his face with a hand. He was in deep waters.

He'd have to keep his distance for the next few days. Parting would be easier that way. If only his heart would quiet its aching.

Preston asked for a tray in his room and took his time getting out of bed. When at last he descended the staircase, the only sounds he heard were the soft footsteps of the servants at work clearing away the morning's activities. The weather was rather agreeable, so perhaps he'd start his day out of doors again.

Just as he reached the entryway door, Mother's voice stopped him.

"Preston, darling. Where have you been all morning?"

"I'm afraid I overslept," he replied, greeting her with a sideways hug. "What have I missed?" *And where is Caroline?*

"Let's see. You missed breakfast. Thomas had business to attend to this morning with his father, and Caroline is out on a ride with Mr. Valcourt. Again." Mother lowered her eyes at him. "Mrs. Avery and I are heading into town for a bit of shopping, if you'd like to join us?"

Preston raised a brow. "No, thank you. I think I shall take a walk, enjoy the sunshine this afternoon."

Mother straightened his cravat. "Take your hat then, dear. You know the sun does nasty things to your scars."

"Indeed." Preston made to turn, decidedly sans hat. His scars couldn't possibly get any worse.

Out the door he went, into the bright afternoon. He cut across the grass, which was crisp under his boots. The wind was just heavy enough to ease the warmth of the day. He had nowhere to go, and all the time to get there, but soon enough he found his feet heading in the direction of the pond where he'd sat last night. What's more, he was not alone when he arrived at the bank.

"Mr. Hubert, how do you do?" he asked.

The man turned around with a start to greet him. "Oh, Mr. Blake. Forgive me, I did not hear you coming. I am quite at odds, actually."

Preston tried to follow the path of Mr. Hubert's gaze, straight out toward the swimming ducks. "Is something amiss?"

"Unfortunately, it is. It seems the attacker has struck again. But this time, it was Romeo's sister who met misfortune." Mr. Hubert pointed out toward a bigger duck with brown feathers and white under its tail. Preston's stomach sank. Sure enough, a large chunk of feathers was missing from her back. "I caught her this morning, and she seemed well despite the bite. I simply cannot account for the predator."

Preston rubbed his jaw, eyes wandering mindlessly around the pond. "What can be done?"

"Normally a duck or two would not cause me too much pause, but now I am invested in the game of it. Why has the animal not succeeded in taking a duck? It cannot be a fox; they are far too clever to fail. It is a puzzle indeed, I'm afraid. As far as what can be done, I can ask the gamekeeper to set a few traps, see what we get," Mr. Hubert said.

Preston nodded his head in approval, grateful that the old groomsman cared so much for Caroline. "Something is better than nothing. I shall keep a close eye out."

Mr. Hubert frowned. "I'll ask you to relay the update to Miss Avery as well, if you would, sir."

Caroline? Preston blinked and stared back dumbly at Mr. Hubert. He'd planned to keep her at a farther distance than Lucifer. "Oh, well . . . perhaps she'd prefer to hear the news from you. After all, you're the one who discovered the new attack."

"No, no," Mr. Hubert answered hastily. "I am sure you are capable of more sensitivity on the matter than I. If you'll excuse me, Mr. Blake. I've work to attend to in the stablehouse."

Preston considered offering his services in the stables in exchange for facing Caroline, but before he'd thoroughly convinced himself that mucking stalls was worth the trade, Mr. Hubert was too far away.

Preston was alone with his thoughts. What was he so worried about, having to face Caroline? She was out with Valcourt. Again. They were as near to courting as a pair could be, while Preston stood alone on the bank of the pond.

Avoiding Caroline was more for his own benefit than hers, and he'd been through worse in his lifetime than heartbreak. He'd find a way to tell her about the ducks then sink back against the wall where he belonged.

An ever loyal, watchful friend.

A BEAUTIFUL LOVE

~

Mr. Valcourt had called on Caroline nearly a dozen times since standing up with her in Preston's place, more frequently this past week than before. He was set to return to London in a few days' time, and Caroline worried she'd led him to believe she was more interested in a proposal than she actually was. Mama's encouragement had been a driving force in her accepting so many calls. But a lifetime with the man? Caroline was truthfully quite lonely in Valcourt's company as he did little to stir her heart. Worse, she was *bored*.

But who wouldn't be interested in a future earl? Would she be mad to discourage a man like Valcourt? He was wealthy enough, to be sure. But their afternoons were always so formal. Like two people wearing only the best versions of themselves. Even if she could train her heart to care for him, how long could she keep that charade going? What would he think of the girl inside her who rescued ducks and battled off a nefarious goose?

Dressed for dinner in a violet gown, Caroline descended to the drawing room. She was the first to enter, so she perched on the pianoforte bench and fingered the ivory keys.

As her fingers stretched up and down the scales in preparation for a song, she pictured herself as a child, just beginning to learn the notes. Back in those days, she, Thomas, and Preston were young and wild. Marriage was barely a thought back then. All the world held for their future was the moment in front of them, and that moment was usually contained in something mischievous.

She started to play the Mozart piece in front of her, and soon she was lost in the music. Page after page consumed her. Mozart was challenging and refreshing, just what Caroline needed.

"You've improved," Preston said, and the music from Caroline's fingertips ceased. She should've expected him to come down for dinner, but he'd surprised her all the same.

"Thank you," she answered. Preston moved around to where she sat on the bench, and Caroline instinctively made room for him to sit beside her.

He smiled as he sat, the space between them on the bench noticeably smaller than in years past. Preston lifted his own hands to the keys and raised his brows. "Hmm, what shall we play?"

Caroline grinned, pretending to think hard on the matter. "Hot cross buns?"

"Hot cross . . ." Preston shook his head with a laugh. "You insult me."

"Pleyel, then?" Caroline shuffled a few pages of sheet music.

"I'll take the top." Preston raised his chin, studying the sonatina in front of them as though he played every day.

A bubble of laughter filled Caroline's chest. His hands were placed entirely incorrectly on the keys. "On my count. One . . . two . . . three—"

The notes wasted no time in accelerating, but it mattered not; Preston was completely lost by the third measure. Caroline slowed her playing to half time. She had to, really, because she could barely breathe for laughter. But the new pace gave Preston just enough time to find his place.

She stole a glance at Preston's face. His eyes were squinted, his head leaned in, and instead of playing with one hand, he was plucking away with both pointer fingers on the upper half of the pianoforte.

"You laugh," he said through his focus. "But the fact that I can still read this at all is quite an impressive accomplishment."

The final two notes were Caroline's, and Preston hurrahed and gave a funny little bow from his seat.

"Well done," she said, lowering the cover over the keys. "I think the pianoforte has had enough for today."

Preston smiled, his countenance falling ever so slightly, and he turned toward Caroline. "I've something to tell you, actually."

An anchor dropped in Caroline's stomach, disrupting a thousand butterflies at its bottom. Was he leaving early? Abandoning her again? "What is it?"

"I do not want you to worry. Hubert and I have discussed a new plan for capturing the predator. But . . . something happened last night."

Caroline immediately stood. Her heart had fallen to her toes. "Romeo."

"He's just fine." Preston stood beside her and held her arms, steadying her. "The same as he was before. It was another duck this time. Just a small patch of feathers gone, like an attempted capture gone wrong."

Caroline shook her head, and her throat thickened. How could this be happening? Was it only a matter of time before one of the ducks was taken? She knew it was silly to love a duck so ardently, but Romeo and his little family filled the empty spaces in her heart. "We have to do something, Preston. We must stop these attacks before . . ." *Before he too is taken from me.*

Preston must've seen the worry on her face, for he pulled her close, enveloping her in his warmth and strength. An energy passed between them, one that seemed to lift all her burdens. She gave her tired hands freedom to fall upon his chest, her cheek to rest upon his shoulder.

"We will stop them," he said in a low voice. His hands moved in calming circles upon her back, and Caroline took a deep breath.

Preston continued, "Hubert and the gamekeeper are setting traps for tonight. I wouldn't be surprised if we have something caught by morning. Rest assured, you are not alone in your worry."

Standing there with Preston, in that moment, she felt anything but alone.

Murmuring from the hallway reached the drawing room door, and slowly, Preston released her, stepping backward.

They stood facing each other as Mama and Father entered with Mrs. Blake, followed closely by Thomas. Caroline patted the right side of her hair smooth, in fear of any disturbance caused by resting it upon Preston. Thomas raised a brow as though she was acting very odd, and heat spread up her neck. What if the whole world could see what she tried so hard to deny? Was her heart written so plainly upon her face?

After quickly greeting Mama with her head low—if anyone would recognize her discomposure it was her—Caroline chose a chair by the hearth and listened to the crackle of its flames for a few minutes. Soft conversation continued on at the front of the room, but Caroline felt anything but content. She tried breathing deeply, crossing and uncrossing her ankles, and even smoothing out every wrinkle in her skirts. Still, her nerves tightened. She had such little control over the things that truly mattered to her. She could not walk the fields in the dark of night searching for danger. She did not know how to set traps or track footprints.

Preston appeared above her. "May I escort you in for dinner?"

Caroline nodded. She couldn't even keep her heart from begging for a man that would never be hers.

"I can tell your mother you are ill if you are worried about the ducks," he whispered as she rose. "You could retire early."

"It's not so much that." Caroline swallowed as she laced her arm through his.

"No?" Preston shot her an inquisitive glance.

No, you blind, handsome man. I love you. "No."

Preston looked as though he was thinking through a great puzzle as they made their way into the dining room. Between Romeo's troubles and Caroline's own heartache, she could hardly stomach her pea soup, nor her roasted lamb. Preston sat across from her, and every time she looked up from her plate, he fought for her gaze.

"And we cannot forget the Rueschs' ball Thursday next," Mama was saying to Mrs. Blake. "We've secured your invitations with the assumption you'll join us."

Mrs. Blake politely chewed her bite of rosemary potatoes before glancing hesitantly to Preston. "A ball sounds very agreeable. Does it not, Preston?"

Caroline's fork froze in midair. She hadn't considered

the ball. Would Preston attend? And if so, would he dance with her at last?

Preston cleared his throat and offered a small smile. "I am confident you will all have a very agreeable time."

"Will you not come?" Thomas asked.

"Oh, do come," Mama prodded.

Preston met Caroline's gaze for so slight a moment, she almost missed it. Could he see her begging, too? There was a pause in the room while eyes watched and ears waited. Thomas caught her gaze and nodded his head toward Preston.

"Come with us," she said. "You owe me a dance, after all."

Preston looked around, clearly uncomfortable. He took a small drink from his cup and wiped his face with a napkin. When he finally spoke, his voice was low but kind. "I have not attended a ball in some time. And I have no plans to. I believe I will be more comfortable here for the evening."

Caroline's fork fell upon her plate with a loud bang, startling even herself. Preston reached out instinctively but retracted his hand.

Heat smoldered to her ears and the emotion in her throat threatened to overflow. Of course Preston would not attend. For some reason, he held tightly to the scars upon his face, like a turtle under the weight of its heavy shell.

"Excuse me," Caroline said in a quaky voice, standing from her seat. Preston was practically abandoning her all over again, and she had to get away before anyone saw the tears pricking at her eyes.

"Dearest, what is the matter?" Mama called after her.

"Let her go," Father answered.
Preston, however, said nothing.

∽

"I HAVE NOT RAISED SUCH a stubborn, impossible man." Mother shook her head with pursed lips and fierce eyes. "Where is your gratitude? Your humility?"

Preston sat on his bed, untying his cravat and unbuttoning his shirt. "I am grateful, Mother. But going to that ball would be like accepting a poisonous flower. As kind as the gesture is, I do not want nor need the gift. It would only hurt me."

Mother paced to his bedside table. "So you will hurt another? Is that how I've taught you to solve your problems?"

"I beg your pardon?"

"Don't be daft with me, son. That girl loves you, and you know it as well as I that you love her too."

Now Preston was standing, heart racing in his chest. He hadn't allowed himself to hope that Caroline's affection matched his own. What good would it do? He swallowed, trying to think of something to say to deny Mother's accusations. But he couldn't.

Mother held Preston's Galen's cream in her hands and motioned to his back. "For too long you have cared what others think or say about these scars. I understand that fate has given you a difficulty that cannot easily be dismissed. But your life is right in front of you."

Preston took off his shirt, and Mother stood behind him, rubbing cool cream upon his back. "Those things are all easy to say..."

"I know what loss feels like, Preston. I know what it is to mourn. These pains, these feelings that you have about what your life should have been. They will not go away. But you must continue living."

How?

The life Preston pictured for himself was as clear in his mind as the doorway in front of him. He'd have married Caroline. He'd have afforded her every luxury and touted her around Town to every possible event Society offered just to show her off. They would wake up together every morning and lie in bed far too long. She would make calls to all their friends. He would see to the estate. Happiness wouldn't do justice to the life they'd have made together.

But his face. His mind. The visions he saw at night when he closed his eyes of fires burning and people screaming for help. None of it fit into a normal life. Caroline deserved better, even if she didn't understand it yet.

Mother finished applying the cream, and Preston dressed in bedclothes. It was late, nearly midnight, but he knew he wouldn't be able to sleep with thoughts such as these.

"I love you, Preston. Your father and I have only ever wanted your happiness. I say these things not because I wish to choose your course for you, but because I do not want opportunities for your happiness to slip away."

Mother kissed Preston's forehead and smiled at him.

"Thank you, Mother," he said softly.

When the door closed shut, Preston sat up in his bed, leaning his head against the wall behind his bedframe. Mother was right. He loved Caroline still. He always would.

But he was a broken man. How could he ask her to live as he did?

The answer was simple: he couldn't.

CHAPTER 5

The traps were empty the next morning and the next, much to the dismay of Preston and Mr. Hubert. So on their third night of trapping, the gamekeeper tried a simple net trap near the pond. Instead of the predator, they caught Lucifer.

"Forgive me, old friend." Hubert laughed as he cut the rope, freeing the hissing goose. "You are not who we are looking for."

"What else can we do?" Preston was teetering on the line between frustration and anger. He knew neither Mr. Hubert nor the gamekeeper was inept. What were they doing wrong?

"It's been three nights without a sign, Mr. Blake. Perhaps we scared the thing off for good." Mr. Hubert wrapped the rope from the trap around the length of his arm and shoulder.

"What if we didn't?" Anger was winning.

"Whatever it is cannot be too great a threat. Nothing is dead, and quite frankly, a lack of tracks is not necessarily a bad sign." Mr. Hubert bowed. "If the Averys need anything further, I am sure they will direct me."

Preston raked a hand through his hair. There was nothing further he could do.

He'd made another promise to Caroline he couldn't keep.

Not that they were on speaking terms anyway. Since dinner three nights ago, she'd appeared for every meal, but vanished directly after, leaving him no time to speak with her alone.

What would he say, anyway? *I am sorry for disappointing you again. I'm sorry I cannot be the man you wish me to be. I want to go back to before, but I cannot.*

His days at the pond and the evening spent checking on the traps had eased his mind in the sense that he could at least soothe Caroline's heart in another way.

But he could not argue with Hubert. Romeo and his family were happy. And alive.

Instead of his usual day out of doors, Preston retreated into the house alone, stressed and uneasy. Mother's voice, mixed with Mrs. Avery's, carried from the drawing room, so he continued walking. The library down the hall would suffice for a temporary hideaway. He needed a moment to breathe.

Curtains were drawn open at full scale, setting the room ablaze with sunlight. Preston nodded to a maid dusting the shelves and, after retrieving a book on horticulture—every man's estate needed to look its best, after all— he fell into a chair and tried to relax.

But the sun was too bright. His book was shadowed, and his eyes were pained from the piercing light in his peripheral vision. He closed his eyes and laid his head back. The insides of his eyelids were painted red from the sun, and Preston instinctively thought of fire.

A woman screamed.

Preston jumped up. The sound reverberated in the room, coming from the corner of the library. The maid.

A loud crash sounded, followed by a boom that silenced the screaming. The room moved in circles in Preston's mind and transformed into a house. A small house with one room.

It was happening all over again. Smoke filled Preston's nostrils, drying his throat into a desert. His mind went black, his vision clouded, and his legs were leaden as he lunged forward desperately to find the woman.

To save her.

She is hurt. She is hurting. He could see no fire, but his body burned, and his throat ached to breathe. He dropped to his knees, pulling wildly at his cravat.

"Help," croaked the small voice. "My legs."

Crawling, Preston reached out to find her, but his limbs were failing him, shaking with both desperation and fear. "I'm coming . . . I'm . . . coming." He couldn't stand the heat. He fingered the buttons on his shirt. His skin would burn again. He'd not recover this time. He couldn't save her.

"Preston?" Mother's voice filled his ears. She did not belong here.

"Go," he told her. "Get out of here."

He felt her arms wrap around him.

"Oh, Winifred!" Mrs. Avery squealed from a distance. "You poor thing, what happened?"

"No." Preston's voice was a whine. Could they not all see? They would burn alive in here.

"I fell from the ladder," the small voice said. "And it followed me. My legs are stuck."

Mother held Preston's face between her hands. His eyes were focusing, but she wasn't real. She couldn't be. Not here. "You are all right, darling. There is no fire. Breathe. I am here."

Another hand grabbed his. A smooth, perfect hand. Caroline.

"What is happening?" came her soft voice.

"He's confused," Mother whispered. "It happens occasionally. It must've been the maid's fall. You stay. I'm going to fetch him something to drink."

It isn't real.
It isn't real.
It isn't real.

~

"Preston?" Caroline's heart was racing as her trembling hands searched for something to do, some part of Preston to hold and fix. She thought of what Mrs. Blake had said and repeated the words. "Everything is all right. There is no fire here."

Preston pulled away from her and covered his face with his hands. Mama and another servant were helping Winifred out of the room. Caroline searched Preston for any sign of exterior wounds. His shirt was hanging open, unbuttoned. Why?

She knew asking questions would be of no benefit yet, but she also didn't know what to say that might help him. He was as still as a board, taking deep breaths. Caroline's heart ached to be near him. Gently she touched his arm. He flinched but did not pull away. So she inched closer, until she could fit her arm along his back.

His breathing grew even, and Caroline rested her chin on his shoulder. After a moment, he leaned in beside her, and she wrapped her arms around him fully. Preston leaned his head upon hers. He wiped his eyes with the palms of his hands and cleared his throat.

"I'm here," Caroline said as calmly as she could. "I cannot imagine your pain, but I am here."

"I'm sorry," Preston breathed. "I'm so sorry you're here."

Caroline reared back to face him, though he would not see her. "I am not sorry. I am glad to be beside you." Her eyes fell to his chest and to his left side which was more badly scarred than his jaw, and her face felt as hot as tea. "However, if you're going to take off your clothes, we really should consider getting you to your bedchamber."

Preston looked up suddenly, then back down to his shirt, and Caroline forced a weak smile. "Here," she said, straightening his shirt and buttoning the top few buttons. She reached behind them for his jacket while he finished the last few buttons and helped him into it.

Preston's stiff movements told Caroline that he likely wanted to escape. And for good reason. How had she gone so long without realizing the fire lived on in his mind? She knew he was uncomfortable, but now more than ever she wanted him to know how much she cared. How dear he was to her.

Preston stood and helped Caroline to her feet.

"Would you like to join me on a walk to the pond? Or on a ride?" she asked, squeezing his arm.

He averted his gaze, taking a step backward. "I—um. No, I think I should rest."

"Of course. Whatever you need."

Preston rubbed the back of his neck, holding his loose cravat in the other hand. His voice was low and thick. "You must think me mad."

"Preston, no. Not in the least." Caroline took a step closer.

"Did you see . . . everything?" His eyes were the most vulnerable she'd ever seen them.

"Just the very end," she answered. She'd seen him tugging at his shirt, begging in a broken voice for his mother to leave him there.

Preston nodded his head solemnly. "I didn't know where I was. Perhaps I *am* mad."

Caroline thought for a moment. She didn't know what it was like to experience something as horrific as what Preston had, but she knew the shock of seeing something difficult and wishing she could unsee it.

"Did you know I watched Romeo hatch from his shell?" Caroline rushed, trying to get the words out before Preston thought her insensitive. "It was a beautiful morning, and I'd ran out without my pelisse when Father told me the ducks had hatched. All but Romeo, that is. I made it just in time. And instantly adored him."

Preston offered her a half smile, so she continued, "But the morning I found him hurt was entirely different. I can remember exactly how the grass smelled—a bit musty and sharp, like metal. The air was chilly, almost wet, and I remember the birds weren't singing. If I close my eyes, I can still see him there in the middle of the grass. His feathers were everywhere. His body was bloodied and torn. I had never seen such a sight, and it was entirely shocking."

Caroline took Preston's hand in hers. "Even sometimes now, when I am out walking, I look out among the grass and my mind tricks me into believing I'll see him there. That I'll see feathers or worse. So I can only imagine what you see when you close your eyes. When you hear a sound or smell a scent."

Preston squeezed her hand, looking down.

"You are not mad." Caroline lifted his hand to her lips and kissed his knuckles. "You are brave and strong and resilient."

"Sometimes I wonder if the fire made me less brave." Preston gave a weak smile. "I didn't think twice when I realized the family was trapped inside with a fire burning out the front room. The mother and four children were trapped in the back room without a window to escape from. The father was already working in my orchards."

Caroline stilled, listening. She wanted him to go on, so she stroked his hand with hers.

"The door was locked, so I tried to shield my face and rammed through with my left side. I fell right into the flames." Preston's eyes were distant. "But I couldn't stop. Not knowing the family was trapped inside. We covered the children in blankets and I carried them out. Their mother wouldn't wait. I begged her—" he cleared his throat. "I begged her to wait. My boots were thick and offered some protection against the hot floor, but she wasn't wearing shoes. She made it out, but . . . not long after, infection set in, and the doctors had to amputate."

Caroline's eyes closed tight. She could hardly bear to

hear of the accident. But Preston lived it again and again. How did he bear it?

"You did everything you could," she whispered. "You saved them. To live through all of that . . . you are the very definition of bravery, Preston."

A bustling sound came from the corner and Caroline turned to see two servants lifting the ladder back into place upon the bookshelf.

"Thank you." Preston's voice was soft. He bowed over her hand and paused a moment before releasing it. "I hope to believe you one day."

Caroline's shoulders fell as Preston crossed the room to the door. His mother stood waiting with a glass of tea in her hands. After whispering something to Preston and kissing his cheek, she let him pass her by before walking into the room.

"Are you shaken?" she asked Caroline, directing her to a nearby settee. "I was the first time I found him like that."

Caroline took her seat. Her mind was whirling, trying to make sense of what she'd just witnessed. "How often are his episodes?"

"Much less than they were. It's been . . . three months? More, since he thought he was back in the fire."

"I had no idea . . ." Caroline swallowed.

Mrs. Blake shifted toward her. "Why do you think Preston keeps to his estate? And distances himself from everyone he cares about?"

Caroline shrugged her shoulders in a rather unladylike fashion. "I suppose he is uncomfortable with what others think when they see him."

"I think you are right," Mrs. Blake said warmly. "And

worse, I think when they speak, he *believes* them. Any time Society tells him he is ugly, or unwelcome, or unworthy of their time, instead of brushing them off like he normally would, Preston accepts their judgements. Seeds have taken root within him, and he does not believe he is deserving of the happiness he, like we all, wishes for."

"That is absurd." Caroline's eyes widened, her head shook in disagreement. "No one of any substance would hear his story and speak ill of him."

Mrs. Blake tsked. "You'd be very surprised."

"I cannot fathom it," Caroline said. "He is too good a man."

"I agree wholeheartedly." Mrs. Blake smiled and stood from her seat. "I think he often worries that his life is too difficult to share. He cares very much for you, you know."

Caroline looked up. A familiar aching in her chest resurfaced, and she wanted to tell Mrs. Blake that she'd tried to make amends with Preston. She'd spoken out of turn, brashly even, to hear his explanation so that she could give hers. But nothing had come of it.

After Mrs. Blake took her leave of the room, Caroline stayed. She sat alone in the library staring at the spot where Preston had leaned into her. He hadn't lied; he was a broken man. But he was still Preston. And if he cared for her as his mother suggested, if there was even a chance they could sort out a future, Caroline would try.

CHAPTER 6

Preston's headache was finally abating, thanks to the salts Mother had brought him when he woke. He'd skipped both dinner last night and breakfast this morning. What would he say to Caroline when he saw her again? He could only imagine where her thoughts had led her since the previous afternoon.

He'd tried to warn her. She deserved better than he was capable of giving her. His mind was just as scarred as his body.

Hiding away protected him from the pitying glances he'd surely receive, but he grew tired of the four walls of his room. He needed to stretch his legs, his back, his neck. Too much sitting caused stiffness and aches that he did not wish to suffer through further. And, he admitted with a heavenward gaze, he wanted to see Caroline. He wanted to know how she would react to him. Perhaps after a good walk, he'd find her.

Preston moaned and rubbed his sore left shoulder as he walked the path to the pond. Fresh air was good for his lungs, and he'd grown fond of the little ducks. No news from Hubert had reached him, though he supposed he'd been a bit preoccupied.

So preoccupied that he hadn't noticed the figure only a few yards ahead of him until it was too late to retreat.

"Preston!" Caroline waved him over. She was sitting at the pond's edge with something in her lap. Her hair was only half pinned up. The rest dangled down her back onto her white day dress.

Preston's nerves surfaced, but he kept walking toward her. Wasn't facing Caroline what he had wanted? Avoiding her would be easier than joining her by a long shot. But he'd see her tonight at the very latest, and an evening gown was much more intimidating than a day dress.

He gave her his best smile as he approached, noting the pencil and notebook she possessed. "Sketching?"

Caroline narrowed her eyes at him, as though waiting for him to poke fun at her. "Yes. Join me, won't you?"

Preston took in a deep breath. Caroline was a good friend. No, an excellent friend. She knew how to navigate a situation of great discomfort and did it flawlessly. He sat down beside her. "Might I see?"

"Not until he is finished."

"Let me guess," Preston's lips twitched. "Romeo?"

Caroline raised her chin, flicking him a glance full of censure. "I'll have you know this is his first portrait."

Preston chuckled, already more at ease than he thought possible. "I see."

"And how are you feeling today?" Caroline asked with her eyes focused on the page in her lap.

"Rested." Preston couldn't help but study the little

wrinkle in her brow and the way she bit her lip as she worked. "Wishing I'd have locked the library door behind me yesterday."

Caroline smirked at Romeo's portrait. "I haven't seen you with your shirt half-off since you were a boy."

Warmth flooded Preston's neck, and he rubbed his cheeks. Which was more embarrassing? That she saw him in such a state or that she spoke of it so freely? "I cannot believe I tried taking off my shirt."

Caroline laughed. "Do not fret, Preston. I only peeked ... well, a few times."

What he could only assume was a horrified expression upon his face only served to make her laugh harder.

"Caroline!" Preston laughed through the reprimand, throwing a handful of grass at her. Heavens, could the woman ever be serious? She fell back onto her elbows, curling into herself with laughter.

"I am sorry," she said on a breath. "We did promise to be honest with one another."

"Is your portrait finished, then?" Preston snatched the book from her lap, and she did not try to stop him. Flipping to the page, he immediately recognized the little duck. Caroline had drawn him just as he was—wounded and broken.

"I think he would approve," Caroline said, staring off at the pond.

"He most certainly would." Preston allowed himself a moment to admire her. His beautiful friend who saw the worth of a person, or a duck, beyond their appearance, and did not wish to manipulate the truth.

Could Mother be right? Was it possible that his future did not have to be as bleak as he imagined?

Preston straightened his position, laying Caroline's book between them. "I am surprised to see you home. Has Valcourt not called today?"

"He has," Caroline answered dismissively. "But I told him I was making last minute preparations for the ball tomorrow night."

The ball. He'd forgotten. He was set to return home in two days' time.

"I wasn't entirely honest with him, but he wouldn't have liked the truth." Caroline scrunched her nose.

"Which is?" Preston prodded.

"Well, I wanted to stay close to home. In truth, I worried after you."

Precisely what he hadn't wanted. "Caroline, those episodes are rare..."

"I wasn't worried you'd take off your shirt again, Preston." Caroline humbled him with a look. "I only wished to be available should you need a friend. Someone to talk to. Or someone to distract you."

Preston thought of several good ways he'd like to be distracted by Caroline. None of which would do either of them any good. He sniffed. "I confess I am not disappointed."

"You do not like him?" Caroline grinned. "Tell me your opinion at once."

Get out of this, man. It's a trap. Preston's mind reached for a change in subject. Things were going so well between him and Caroline. Indeed, she was the one person who saw him for who he really was. But he'd promised her honesty. Hadn't he wanted to warn her off Valcourt?

He picked at the grass, trying to choose his words

carefully. He could tell the truth without being unkind, after all. "Valcourt . . . seems like someone who would enjoy . . . the lifestyle of an earl . . ."

Caroline raised a brow. "You *don't* like him."

"No!" Preston rushed, his mind racing wildly for an excuse. But he had none. Blast it all, he could not lie. "That is to say . . . no. I cannot say that I have much regard for the man."

"You've only met him in passing," Caroline argued. The sound in her voice was not convincing. "He has . . . some redeeming qualities."

Preston huffed. He might as well get it all done with. "Valcourt is a critical fop, Caroline. And you are a beautiful woman whom he does not deserve in the least."

Caroline broached a catlike smile. "You've never called me beautiful before."

"Of course I have," Preston said defensively. Caroline was the most beautiful woman he'd ever seen. He'd told her, hadn't he?

"That, I'd have remembered." Caroline smiled to herself. "Edwin speaks of my appearance so much I can hardly tell whether he is being genuine or merely wishes to flatter me."

Preston grimaced. She'd used Valcourt's Christian name. As far as Preston was concerned, anything that snake said or did was only for personal gain. Something about him irked Preston beyond simple dislike.

He stretched out his hands, flexing the muscles in his arms. One step out of line, and he'd rather enjoy showing Valcourt a thing or two about fisticuffs. Caroline was far above him, earl or not.

"Will he be at the ball tomorrow evening?" Preston couldn't help but ask.

Caroline shot him a sideways glance. "Yes. In fact, he asked to escort me, but I'd assumed at the time you would be attending, so I offered him my regrets."

Blast it all. She'd rejected her suitor for him. Any man in his right mind would take that as enough encouragement to drop everything at her feet and beg for a chance. Preston's mind, however, was anything but normal. He was neither as wealthy as Valcourt nor as elevated in status. And his appearance . . . well, he'd be Caroline's ugliest suitor by far.

But he loved her. How he loved her.

All of these thoughts mulled around in his mind until his palms were sweaty and he imagined the ballroom full of staring eyes and whispering voices.

"Pity," was all he could say in return.

"Indeed," Caroline agreed.

The pair of them sat together in thought watching the ducks swim freely in the pond. Occasionally one would drop down under the water and Preston would follow around with his eyes until the creature popped back up a few feet away. The water rippled from the light breeze, and Preston watched the lines smooth out toward the bank. It was oddly soothing.

"Preston?" Caroline grabbed his arm suddenly. Her back straightened and she peered out toward the brush a few yards away. "What is that?"

Searching for any sign of movement, Preston pulled himself to a kneeling position.

"There!" Caroline pointed hastily, and Preston

followed her finger to the source. It was black and hairy and very much out of place.

The predator.

Preston jumped to his feet. "Stay here," he told Caroline. The form had already vanished, but if he ran, he could follow its path into the pasture. He might at least get a better glimpse of it.

Rushing to the spot where the black mass had flashed, Preston found nothing. He must've run for a quarter mile in pursuit before stopping to check his surroundings. The pasture he'd fled to was still, save for singing birds in the treetops. What sort of creature with black fur would attack ducks? A stout? No, that wouldn't be it. A badger was a more likely threat, but Preston wasn't convinced.

Cursing his failure, Preston retreated to the pond at a slow pace, searching the ground for any tracks. Whatever it was, the animal was small and light on its feet. He found Caroline in the grass, decidedly not staying put as he'd asked her to.

"Preston, come quickly," she said as he approached. "Look at this."

Preston jogged to where she crouched and joined her. She was pointing to a marking in the earth. A small four-fingered pawprint.

"Have you seen anything like this before?" she asked, looking hopefully up at him.

"I wouldn't know," he answered truthfully. "But Hubert will."

～

TONIGHT WAS THE NIGHT. Caroline could feel it in her bones. Though he couldn't name the creature with certainty, Hubert had set three new traps after seeing the markings Caroline and Preston found. Nothing had come during the day. Knowing the predator had been watching her sweet ducks, Caroline winced. It would likely be back tonight.

She'd tried to close her eyes, but her pillow was hard as a rock, and she was sure new lumps had formed in her bed. She was too warm, then too cold, and the moon was far too bright shining through her curtains. What time was it anyway? Would morning never come?

Caroline walked to the window, drawing back her curtains and peering out into the night. She couldn't see the pond from where her window angled, but she searched her view regardless.

She perched on the window sill, leaning her head against the glass, and closed her eyes.

She'd just started to drift when a roaring sound, a howl, carried in the wind. Caroline's eyes popped open, her heart leapt into her chest. What—who—was out there? Was it near Romeo?

Wringing her hands together, Caroline paced the floors of her room. What could she do? Lucifer stood guard, and for once she was grateful the old goose knew how to defend himself.

But he hadn't stopped the attacks before. Nothing had. Not even the traps.

Before she knew what she was doing, Caroline lit a candle and knotted her hair into a loose bun atop her head. She pulled out her pelisse from the armoire and tugged on her boots. Candle in hand, she slowly turned the knob on her door and crept out into the hallway.

No one. Silence.

She barely closed the door behind her, not wanting to make a sound. If Father caught her out alone at night, she'd be in more trouble than she could say. But if anything happened to Romeo...

She crept down the hallway until light from under a doorway caught her attention.

Preston's room.

Was he awake at this hour? She paused for a moment, listening. There was no one but her in the hallway. The house was indeed still.

She knocked lightly three times and whispered, "Preston?"

Movement from within the room caused her to step back. He was awake. The door crept open, and Preston appeared in the crack with his own candle in hand. "Caroline? Are you well?"

Caroline took him in. His thin, loose nightshirt, the disarray of his hair. His scars were evident, more so than ever before, and her eyes followed them down his face, his neck, his sinewy chest. She imagined tracing her way to his shoulders and feeling the strength in his arms that had held her, kept her safe.

He cleared his throat.

Caroline's cheeks were lit with fire, and she remembered her resolve. She took in a quick, shallow breath. "Did you hear that sound earlier?"

Preston braced himself against the doorframe. "I am sure it was only the wind."

Caroline took a conscious step nearer and lowered

her voice. "What if it wasn't? What if Romeo is in danger? I cannot bear it."

"You are dressed for out of doors." Preston eyed her, taking her measure. "Certainly, you do not mean to go out alone."

"Come with me." Caroline leaned in, tugging at his hand. A flood of warmth passed through her. "You promised to help me keep him safe. Please, Preston. I cannot sleep until I see that he is well."

Preston drew a hand through his already ruffled hair and studied her face. She was in earnest, surely he could see that.

"It wouldn't be proper. Just as this"—he motioned to her standing in his doorway— "is far from proper."

Caroline frowned at him, huffing out air from her nose. "Fine. Then I shall go alone."

What had she been thinking asking Preston for help? When would she learn that he clearly only meant to be her friend? She made to turn but was stopped by his hand.

"Wait," he said, tugging her back. He shook his head as though he couldn't believe he was saying the words. "Let me get my boots."

～

THE NIGHT AIR was much chillier than Caroline had anticipated. Her night dress was far too thin, even covered by her pelisse, but at least the quickness of their pace toward the duck pond kept her blood flowing. Preston was quiet. He hadn't offered her his arm or his jacket, nothing that would connect them. While she knew he was only trying to be honorable, she would've appreciated his warmth.

His lantern was bright enough for both of them to see the path at their feet, and the moonlight lit the rest of the earth enough to ease Caroline's fears. When at last the pond was in sight, they slowed their movements.

"Let's go around, through the trees," Preston said, pointing off to where they'd seen the animal earlier.

Caroline followed closely behind him but kept her eyes on the pond. Unless her vision failed her, she counted all five little bodies floating around in the moonlight.

Oomphf. Caroline rammed into Preston's back. Why had he stopped? He lifted his hand and crouched.

"For once in your life, Caroline Avery, stay put." His voice was a stern, solemn whisper as he crept forward, leaving the lantern beside her.

Caroline obeyed, for terror had seized her. Silently, she watched as he inched forward. He moved with such stealth, she hardly realized he'd taken off his coat. He was feet from her.

Then he pounced.

"Preston!" she called, standing. He groaned against something beneath him.

"I've got you," he growled. "Stay still, now, I've got you."

Caroline raced forward with the lantern in her hand and knelt beside him. "What is it? What can I do?"

"You never listen," Preston said. He was balling up his coat, which was thrashing around wildly in his arms. "I can't believe I didn't think of this before."

Caroline stood as Preston did, and reached out to the

79

ball of coat. When the creature calmed, Preston laughed. "Caroline, it's a cat."

"What?"

Preston peeked into the coat, and as Caroline lifted the lantern, a small head appeared. A black cat. An adorable little black cat with green eyes.

The weight she'd been carrying, all the fear and worry, instantly dissipated from her shoulders. Caroline took her first easy breath in days.

"I'm afraid he's been quite neglected. He is all bones." Preston cautiously pet the animal's head. It looked ready to pounce, but more desperate than ungrateful.

"He must be starving. Give him to me," Caroline said. Where could they find food, not including duck, that might fill their new friend's stomach for the night?

"Are you honestly going to comfort this cat? You remember he's tried on multiple occasions to eat Romeo and his family." Preston traded the lantern for the bundled coat as the excitement of the previous moment dissipated.

"You *are* bones," she said to the cat as she adjusted it in her arms. "We shall find you some milk in the very least to tide you over for the night."

Preston spoke in obvious disbelief, shaking his head. "I cannot believe it."

"Romeo is safe now," she called back. "This cat will be no threat once his own needs are met. Besides, he is rather adorable."

"Honestly?" Preston walked beside her. They'd reached the path back toward the house but veered off toward the barn. "What will you call him? Tybalt?"

Caroline laughed aloud. "You're being incorrigible. Where is your heart?"

~

How Preston found himself milking a cow in the middle of the night to feed a wayward cat was beyond him. He barely knew where the udders were, let alone how to tug milk from them. But he couldn't deny Caroline. Not with the sad, hopeful face she gave him when she asked. Nor could he deny the satisfaction he felt as the poor little creature happily drank the entire bowl. He filled it once more as Caroline made a bed of straw and a stray blanket in a cozy corner. The wooden, lidded box she found would contain the cat until morning, when Preston could only imagine what plan Caroline would concoct for it.

"He's all tucked in," she said with a happy smile as she brushed off her skirt. She'd never looked more beautiful than she did with muddy boots and dirt on her cheek. Preston picked a few loose straws from her hair and smiled to himself. The woman was incredible. She saved ducks, orchestrated the capture of their predators, and then saved the predators.

"I think we should get you to bed, then. The moon is falling." And he was exhausted.

They stood face to face, and Caroline fidgeted with a button on her pelisse. She was quiet, looking at him with some sort of hesitant amazement. He couldn't begin to account for that look.

She took a few steps closer, only inches from him, and his heart beat in his ears.

There was only the two of them.

Slowly, she wrapped her arms around his neck and pulled him into an embrace. His drowsy arms folded over her and the smell of apples and cinnamon, and now hay, fogged his senses even more.

Caroline.

"Thank you," she whispered in his ear. "For everything."

A gentle kiss on his scarred cheek sent a rush through his entire body. Every careful defense he'd built around his heart crumbled until he was left with nothing but longing to be with Caroline. He leaned into her warmth and they stood together, neither letting go.

"Preston?" she asked in the softest voice. Could she feel the beat of his heart? How it raced for her? "I must know. I'm sorry, but I cannot come to peace without knowing."

"What is it?" he asked into her hair. He needed to go to bed. He needed to leave before a servant came in and saw them like this. Before he moved even closer to this beautiful woman who smelled of apples and made him weak.

"If you hadn't run into that fire . . . would you have kept your promise a year ago?"

It was as though someone had thrown cold water on his face. He reared back, searching her questioning eyes. "Caroline, I would always have run into that fire."

She looked down at his chest sheepishly. "But if you hadn't . . . if there was never a fire in the first place. Would you have come for me?"

Their breaths drew even, and Caroline bit her lip. She was throwing her heart out in front of him. She loved him. His Caroline loved him. But he couldn't move. What he wanted to say would encourage her to believe that more could come from their friendship. He knew more than anyone the pain that came from a connection with him. The pain that came from isolation.

Caroline looked up at him. He'd never seen such vulnerability in her eyes. Fear of being alone in her affection. It was all too much.

Would you have come for me?

"Yes," he answered, tracing her cheek with his hand. "And I'd have never left."

Her eyes changed from helplessness to urgency. "Then why must anything be different? You are the same to me, and if our friendship can come so easily, why can't we—"

Preston hastily released her, stepping back. He couldn't let her misunderstand his words. "But *I* am not the same. My life is not the same. You deserve everything I *meant* to give you." He shook his head. "I am a broken man now, Caroline. You saw what my mind can do. And people see me differently. Most just look away, but others . . . You deserve to be the one Society looks for, and not because of your connection to an ugly man."

"Ugly?" Caroline drew closer. "You are not ugly, Preston. Not to me."

Preston's lips tugged upward. "Of course not to you. To the woman who saves ducks whose feathers are nearly all plucked."

"I am in earnest." Caroline grabbed his coat, and Preston's arms fell weakly to his sides. "If you wish to dissuade me, only tell me you do not care for me."

He rubbed his jaw. She wouldn't hear him. How could

he make her see? Why did he even want to anymore? He lifted her hands in his. "Caroline, I care for you more than anyone in this world. But you have not seen what I have seen. I am not the same man; you must believe me. And you must hear me when I tell you that things between us must stay as they are. Years from now when we're old and your children have children, you will look back and see that your life has been full. That is all I want."

"A full life? How will my life be full without you?" Caroline withdrew from his hold and took his face between her hands as though forcing *him* to hear *her*. "I don't care if we have parties every weekend, or attend every ball, so long as *you* are the one beside me every night."

She bit her lip through a shy smile. "I've loved you since I was a little girl. When I was eight years old and Thomas dared you to kiss me. You did it with a grin on your face, and I knew one day when we were older I'd make you kiss me again. I don't want a full life if it isn't with you."

Preston's breath grew still. How he'd longed to hear those words. To speak them himself. He leaned closer, his heart ablaze, and rested his forehead upon hers. "My dear Caroline. You don't know what you're saying."

Caroline's voice was a whisper. "Do I not? Come to the ball tomorrow. Keep your promise this time and dance with me. If you are as miserable as you say, if Society is cruel and hateful and pitying then I promise, in return, I will accept your wishes and never ask another thing of your heart."

Preston touched his nose to hers. She smiled and

continued. "But if, by chance, you find the evening bearable, then I expect you to call on me the very next day. And every day after."

Could such a thing be? Could he learn to carry this burden with Caroline at his side? Could he ask so much of her?

"I don't want to hurt you again," he breathed.

"Then come." Caroline pushed back from his embrace and grinned. "I'll wear my blue dress and you can admire me until you've the bravery to ask me to dance yourself."

Preston returned her grin. Gads, if he didn't love her with all his heart. But he knew how the night would end. That she would see that what he described was reality, not despondency.

She needed to see.

His heart was full and breaking at the same time. "Might I escort you, then?"

CHAPTER 7

*C*aroline sat upon her vanity bench staring at her reflection in the mirror. Something was wrong.

No, everything was wrong.

Dabbing frantically at her lips with a cloth, she pushed Martha away with her free hand. "It's too bright, Marty. I look like an over-rouged mistress."

A knock sounded on her door.

"Dearest, we are waiting in the foyer for you. Fashionably late is near past if we do not leave at once," Mama said from the other side. Patience was wearing thin in her voice.

Caroline tried to take a deep breath, but her ribs would not open. She let out a frustrated huff at Martha. "My dress is too tight. My hair is . . . flat. We are not ready. Tell Mama I need more time."

But the door opened of its own accord. "Do not speak to our dear Martha so. No more primping. The carriage is leaving in five minutes, with or without you, my love."

"But, Mama—"

"Loosen her stays a touch, if you will Martha. She's not thinking clearly." Mama raised a brow and swept from the room.

Marty chewed on her bottom lip. Caroline wanted to scream into her pillow. One night was all she had to convince Preston that together, society could be bearable for him. Everything needed to be perfect, down to the very last strand of her hair.

Marty's fingers glided over her lacings. "Forgive me for saying so, miss. But you seem a bit out of sorts. Perhaps we should focus less on your appearance and take a moment to just . . . breathe."

Her stays loosened, and Caroline's shoulders slackened as air flew into her lungs. Leaning against the post of her bed, she closed her eyes and tried to clear her head. *It's just a dance. Just one night.*

"Rumor has it, Mr. Blake is just as nervous as you are."

Caroline's jaw dropped, and she reared back to stare at her maid.

Marty smiled her crooked smile. "He went through a dozen knots on his cravat before he settled on the right one. His man is belowstairs with his fingers in the ice bucket."

Caroline giggled and Marty joined in. "Preston, nervous? I don't believe you."

"Indeed, he is. And I'd wager waiting anxiously below for you to descend."

A wave of guilt crested in Caroline's chest. What was all this for, anyway? Preston wouldn't care if her hair was flat or her Rose Salve too rosy. "Thank you, Marty. I hope you'll forgive my nerves for being so overbearing tonight. I don't know what's come over me."

"Let's get you laced up then," Marty said, moving behind Caroline once more.

~

"She's on her way down," Mrs. Avery said as she descended the staircase. "Truly, this time."

Preston let out a small breath. Half an hour they'd been waiting. The carriage was ready, and Thomas had left on his horse to ride with Miss Talent's family. Mr. Avery was reading his paper in a chair by the entryway door.

Mother had been so pleasantly surprised at his last-minute change of heart to attend the ball, she'd not ceased smiling all day. Between Caroline's long hours in her room and Mother's incessant grins, Preston was quite ready to denounce the ballroom altogether. Not to mention how dizzy he felt waiting for Caroline to appear.

His man had doused his hair in wax, fluffing it even more so than usual atop his head. It wasn't quite as terrible as Valcourt's, but it made him feel out of sorts all the same. He checked his reflection in a mirror hung in the foyer. Nothing had changed, despite his nice clothes and fluffy hair. Scars still raked horribly across his left side. The fire still raged in his memory.

"Finally," Mrs. Avery breathed, clasping her hands together.

Preston looked up. His lips parted.

Caroline glowed as she stepped down to meet them.

Dressed in blue silk, her movements were as fluid as a rushing stream. Her gloved hand slid down the bannister, and the ends of her pinned curls brushed the side of her neck.

Preston couldn't move.

Until Mother jabbed him in the side. "Go on," she hissed at him.

Quickly, he cleared his throat, making it just in time to receive her at the bottom of the staircase. "You look . . . lovely." Taking her hand, he managed a bow. Her eyes lit up with a smile.

"Thank you," she said, curtseying back.

Now, what? Preston's mind was a blank slate. Should he stare at her for a moment longer? Bow again? Or suggest they find their seats in the carriage? Was that his place?

"Your hair is different." Caroline's voice was full of teasing and she was forcing down a smile. The rouge on her lips was maddening.

"I hear it's all the rage in London." Preston laced Caroline's hand into the crease of his arm. He noticed movement out of the corner of his eye, and the nod of Mother's head to follow their party to the carriage. "Shall we?"

Caroline giggled. A sound that gurgled from her throat and made Preston laugh aloud. "What is it?" Preston asked as they stepped out the door.

"I'm just . . . excited, I suppose. We've never stood together formally."

"So I must beg you to remember I have not danced a set in a year."

Caroline took his hand and stepped into the carriage. When Preston entered, he took a seat by Mother, opposite Caroline. A footman closed the door behind him, and just like that, the carriage started to roll.

The anticipation in Caroline's eyes sobered him. She obviously had set her heart on the evening's success already. He couldn't blame her. In a perfect world, he'd be pleading just as ardently for a good enough outcome to extinguish his worries. He had to be realistic, though. And realism told him to prepare for the worst. That didn't necessarily mean they couldn't enjoy their dance together. Or a few moments in between.

The ride was shorter than he'd expected. Then again, he'd been well distracted by Caroline's dress grazing against his legs.

Candles and lanterns were lit at every corner of the host's grand estate. Preston did not know the Ross family, but he was extremely grateful to be attending a private party as opposed to an assembly. The numbers would be smaller, and the people hopefully would have better manners than others he'd run into.

Stepping down from the carriage, he found at least a dozen or so guests crowded on the front lawn conversing. He'd have to walk through them to get to the door. Distracting Caroline from seeing their reactions to his face this early was of the utmost importance. He did not want to ruin her night before their dance.

Music carried from the ballroom. Mother and the Averys walked ahead of them down the gravel path toward the entry, and Caroline took his arm without being asked. Hands clammy and warm inside his gloves, Preston drew a little breath and kept walking.

Voices sounded from behind them. A new group of people. More eyes.

". . . the quadrille is the most fun, of course, but I do love a country dance," Caroline was saying. He'd barely had a moment to think of their dance, so worried as he was to just get into the house and finish with introductions.

He lifted his gaze a moment too soon, though. Three ladies stood to his left, their mouths agape with horror. Preston swallowed and nodded, thanking his stars that Caroline's head was turned the other way. He didn't want the night to be ruined before it even began. He was determined to give Caroline a few good memories before her eyes were opened to Society's judgment of him.

"Did you see his face?" One of them said as he passed. Preston's free hand formed a tight ball.

"Good heavens, what could cause such a terrible deformation?"

Caroline tugged him through the door toward an elderly woman with enough feathers in her headdress to cover three Romeos. "Mrs. Edith Ross. She is the grandmother of Galena Ross, in whose honor this party is thrown," she whispered into his ear. Mr. Avery made their introductions, and Mrs. Ross' pursed lips tilted ever so slightly when he bowed to greet her.

"Mr. Preston Blake. I knew your grandfather quite a long time ago. A good man, he was," Mrs. Ross said. Her aged eyes sparkled like diamonds caught in the light.

"Thank you," Preston said a bit taken aback. "I miss him very much."

"Of course you do." She turned to the small woman

standing next to her. "Galena come, Mr. Blake was just asking after a dance."

Preston nearly choked. He threw a worried glance to Caroline, who seemed more amused than perturbed. "Uh—"

Miss Ross stepped forward, her eyes searching his face. She squinted at his left side, frowning.

"I would like that very much, Miss Ross. If you are not opposed." Except he wouldn't like it. Not at all. To be seen standing with the guest of honor. All eyes in the room would be on him. Whispers would start immediately.

"Very well. The quadrille, then," Miss Ross answered with a curtsey. Preston nearly forgot to bow.

Their families moved forward into the ballroom, and Caroline left for a moment to switch into her dancing slippers. Preston stood against a back wall, glancing up at the room. Six sets of eyes. No, ten. They were looking back at him with words on their lips.

Who is that man? What is wrong with him? He'd become good at reading lips from a distance.

"Shall I introduce you to a few of my friends?" Miss Ross had found him. He knew she only meant to be a good hostess, seeking out a man who stood alone against a wall.

"That won't be necessary," he spoke quickly. Miss Ross looked utterly confused. "That is to say, I am unable to stay through the evening. And I leave for my own estate in two days' time. I'd hate to interrupt conversation in vain."

"I see." She looked at him curiously.

Preston searched the room for Caroline. He found her near the edge of the current dancers surrounded by a party of gentleman. Including Valcourt. His eyes were set on her like a hawk to its prey.

"I don't like conversing much, myself," Miss Ross continued. "Grandmother hosts these parties in my honor, though I've begged her to let me be."

Preston could well understand that sentiment and nodded his head. As kind as Miss Ross was, his mind was not engaged. Music had ceased, and Valcourt was leaning in closer to Caroline.

"I believe this is our set," Miss Ross said meagerly.

Preston snapped to attention. Blast it all, she was right. He held out his right arm to her and led her to the dance floor. The quadrille. At least he knew it well from memory.

A body pushed into his shoulder, and Preston tensed. "Pardon—" The man's eyes popped, his voice changing to a frightened sound.

"Excuse me," Preston bowed his head, stepping past the man. A half dozen others had stopped to find the source of the sound, staring at him as he walked on. His neck grew hot. Had Caroline seen?

"Never mind that man," Miss Ross said. "He is new money. Unfamiliar with proper manners and social etiquette."

Preston offered her a grateful smile. "He is not the only one lacking tonight, I'm afraid."

With a hum of the violins and a plucking of strings, the dance started, and Preston took Miss Ross's hand. Their feet moved in circles as they twirled about the floor, switching partners and then back again. Preston was glad to dance with Miss Ross. She was unlike the bulk of Society in that she saw his differences but tossed them aside. Were there others like her did not define worth based on appearance alone?

Miss Ross smiled as their steps led them back together. She was quiet and refined, but she looked at him as though he were any other man.

She reminded him of Caroline.

CHAPTER 8

Caroline sank into a chair. She'd danced for three hours with seemingly every man in the room but Preston. He, on the other hand, had danced with Miss Ross twice, and two other women. Why had he not asked her yet? She had half a mind to walk right up to him and demand the next set. He was here for her, after all. They'd come together.

She couldn't deny the stares. Everyone looked at him. She'd heard the whispers, too. He hadn't lied when he said society was difficult, but he smiled nonetheless. That had to be a good sign, right?

Standing from her seat, she pushed through the crowd to find him. She'd given him more than enough opportunities to ask after a set, but enough was enough. Valcourt was due for another dance and sitting around would only give him an opportunity to ask for it.

She found Preston with his mother standing near a table with punch and a small spread of food. He smiled at her and beckoned her over with a nod.

"You must be exhausted," he said as he poured a glass of punch. "For you."

She took the glass and sipped. "Not quite," she said with a meaningful look that she hoped was inviting enough to warrant a dance.

It was not lost on Preston, who chuckled in return. "Might I claim your next set?"

Caroline heaved an exaggerated sigh. "At last."

Mrs. Blake touched Caroline's arm. "You dear girl. I've told him repeatedly how very rude he's been."

"I haven't wanted to seem overbearing," Preston retorted. "Besides, I have been quite entertained merely watching."

"Go on, then." Mrs. Blake shooed them with her hands. "Dancers are getting in line."

Preston took Caroline's hand and led her forward with purpose. She wondered if his heart was as frantic as hers.

They squeezed in between two other couples, and Preston stepped back a few paces in line with the rest of the men. As they waited for the music to begin, Caroline stole a glance at Preston. He chewed on his bottom lip. Was he nervous? Caroline tried desperately to force down her smile. She'd wanted this so badly, dreamt of this moment for a year, and here she was standing in front of him. Preston looked more regal and more handsome than she'd ever seen him.

Music filled the air and Caroline started a step too late. Preston grasped her hand as he passed her, his fingers lingering on her wrist and sending a jolt to her heart. She took in a small breath and caught his gaze as he circled back. He was laughing, or was at least amused, and it was contagious. He brushed the back of his hand with hers as they turned and grinned.

"Be serious," she whispered, though she felt anything but.

"I am," he replied, never looking away. Caroline's stomach flipped into her chest. His eyes were focused and sweet, and every time the steps brought them together, he grinned unabashedly down at her. So instead of being so serious, Caroline planned the next twirl. When Preston took her hand, she drew closer to him than ever before, her nose mere inches from his. Preston's lips parted as the steps pulled Caroline away again, and his grin changed into something new.

∼

Preston couldn't go back to the way things were. Not after this dance.

The way Caroline pulled him close. The way her eyes smoldered as she watched him. It would be his undoing.

The set was nearly through, but Preston didn't want the music to end. He wanted to hold her hand and watch her twirl and pull her close as they spun together in tandem.

He loved Caroline Avery.

And he intended to do anything in his power to make her happy for the rest of their lives. Would the world accept them together? Could he overlook the stares and whispers? Could she?

He bowed as the music lulled, and Caroline curtseyed in return. He couldn't help but laugh as she said, "Can you believe you missed this the first time?"

"I cannot." What had he been thinking? Why did he care so much about gossip and ridicule when Caroline's opinion, her happiness was all that he truly measured?

"Oh, Preston, I am so glad to hear it..."

Caroline was talking, but Preston's ears were suddenly distracted. Valcourt was a few paces behind them with a lady on his arm. "Not to worry," he was saying. "I cannot imagine his face is contagious..."

Preston's arm flexed. Valcourt was spreading rumors about him. About his scars.

Let him talk. Preston pressed his lips together. He had all he'd ever need right beside him.

Caroline tightened her hold on him, raising her voice. "You must tell me more about your orchards. When is your next harvest?"

But the voices grew louder too. Hateful and disgusted. Preston stared dumbly at his feet, only half-attentive to her question.

"He is hideous," the woman with Valcourt replied. Preston's stomach sank.

"It is a pity," Valcourt continued. "I wouldn't go too near to be safe, if I were you. I only mean to help. I'm not entirely sure what Mrs. Ross was thinking, inviting a creature like that without knowing fully his circumstances."

Preston stopped in his tracks. Caroline looked back at him in haste, clearly worried. Anger spread from his nostrils to his toes. No more would he feel shame or offer apology for his appearance, or for who he was. Caroline was all that mattered now. And he intended to make that known to her first thing in the morning.

Valcourt prattled on he passed by them as though he was completely unaware of Preston's presence. Preston needed air before his fists made him remorseful. "I've forgotten something," he told Caroline. "A handkerchief."

Caroline's brows knit together. She didn't believe him, but he'd have to beg her forgiveness later.

"I'll return in a moment." He nodded her forward. Valcourt aside, the night hadn't been as uncomfortable as he predicted. Not with Caroline so close. The stares and the whispers were there, as usual, but the loneliness he so often felt was abated by her presence. Everything he thought could never be was changing into a beautiful possibility.

That was, as long as he didn't punch a soon to be earl in the nose.

He made his way to the entry, waving off the butler who attended those leaving. He wouldn't need his coat, just a quick breath of fresh air.

Until those same voices caught up with him.

"There he is again," a woman sneered as he passed. "Is he leaving, finally?"

"Look at that face. How does he live?"

"Did you see him dancing with Miss Avery? She almost looked . . . happy. I cannot fathom it."

"Never fear, ladies," Valcourt interjected.

Preston's fingers twitched. His arm ached to follow through. He needed out of this place, and quickly. In all his years, he'd never been so publicly slandered.

A man in front of him paused to adjust his hat, blocking the only way out.

Valcourt continued, "We can all breathe openly again. The monster is leaving at last."

There was no time for thinking. Preston's arm was fueled by the anger and callousness he'd harbored since the fire. Turning, he anchored his focus on Valcourt's nasty smile and swung like his very life depended on it.

A pop cracked the air, and Valcourt fell back cursing. Ladies all around gasped and retreated. Preston's hand pounded with pain that shot up his arm and into his shoulder.

Valcourt hobbled to a standing position and raised his fists.

"That is enough," a man was rushing forward. "Enough!"

Preston lowered his hands as the man came upon them, but Valcourt swung. Preston's jaw burst with pain, blood poured from a gash in his lip, but Preston didn't hesitate. He'd wanted to best this man for too long. Another swing, another punch, and Valcourt was down again.

Arms encircled him, pulling him back. Voices all around were murmuring in shock.

"Enough, Preston," Mr. Avery said fiercely. He held Preston up. "Think of where you are, son."

The very word sobered him. Son. What would his father say, seeing him now?

Valcourt was on his knees surrounded by a dozen men patting his shoulders, and ladies throwing their handkerchiefs at him.

Standing across the hall with her hand over her chest was Caroline. She was pale, as though she'd just lost something dear.

Mrs. Ross approached the two of them. "Mr. Avery, if you do not mind. I must ask you and your guest—"

"Of course, Mrs. Ross," Mr. Avery bowed, pushing

A BEAUTIFUL LOVE

Preston out the door. "Do forgive us. I hope your evening can continue on after this."

Wind cooled Preston's face. His right side ached, for Valcourt had meant to damage the better of him. Mr. Avery's neck was red, his lips were a tight line as he pressed a cloth to Preston's chest and forced him into the carriage.

"I must offer every apology, Mr. Avery," he began after sitting, dabbing the cloth to his bloody lip. "But that man—"

"I heard every word." Mr. Avery sat across from Preston. His hands were fists. "If not for my family's reputation, I'd have pummeled the man myself."

Preston's jaw dropped. "I shouldn't have—"

"You very well should've." Mr. Avery leaned closer. The moonlight fell through the carriage window, lighting the new anger in his eyes. "To treat another man with such disdain is disgraceful. Your father would've been proud to see you defend yourself."

The door to the carriage cracked open, and a footman helped Mother up the stairs. She reached her arms out to him as she took her seat beside him. "My boy. My dear boy."

"Forgive me, Mother," Preston whispered. Mrs. Avery settled in beside her husband, followed by Caroline. What must she think of him now? He couldn't see her face in the dark.

"What a scene," Mrs. Avery sighed as the door closed behind them. "Are you all right, Preston?"

"I believe we should worry more about Mr. Valcourt." Mother patted Preston on the knee.

"He'll recover," Mr. Avery said. Preston leaned his

head against the window. He couldn't say he felt bad about injuring Valcourt. Indeed, he was quite liberated. But he'd hurt Caroline in the process and that was inexcusable.

"Did you see to him before you left, Caroline?" Mrs. Avery sounded like she asked more from curiosity than worry. Still, Preston did not care to know.

Silence filled the open space.

"Caroline?" she asked again.

"He is fine, Mama."

Preston lifted his head. There was sadness in her voice. Grief.

"Leave her be, Laura," Mr. Avery warned.

Mother squeezed his hand, and Preston replayed the night's events in his memory. He'd endured worse back home, but nothing as personal and vindictive as how he'd been treated tonight. And yet, his dance with Caroline had been the happiest moment of his year. How did one differentiate the two? Would there always be bad with the good? Punching Valcourt had been very bad indeed, and yet, the act itself was so liberating. But Valcourt was Caroline's friend, was he not?

No, he should have kept walking. The night would have ended pleasantly. Caroline would have been happy. He could've taken her out for a drive first thing in the morning. Could she ever forgive him?

When the carriage rolled up the drive to Mayberry Park, Preston's muscles tensed. He needed to speak with Caroline alone and beg her forgiveness. He had to make her see that he could live her life without losing his grip at every turn. Now that he knew what it felt like to have her in his arms, he needed her.

"Caroline," he called moving quickly after her. She was nearly running for the house. "Caroline, wait."

She was sniffling, wiping her cheeks with her hands when he reached her. "Let me go, Preston."

Preston's limbs went numb. He'd ruined everything. He'd hurt her even worse than before. "I just—let me explain."

"I heard what he said. I am so sorry," she wiped a loose tear from her cheek. "I understand now. What you said about Society."

The Averys were hovering at the entryway with Mother between them. But Preston needed more time. He needed Caroline to hear him. He'd changed his mind. He wanted the life she'd spoken of, regardless of Society.

"I must go." Caroline lifted her gaze to his. The pain in her eyes was worse than any fire. "Thank you for the dance."

He tried calling out for her again, but his voice failed him. Preston stood alone on the gravel watching the love of his life walk away. His entire body was unsteady, shaking with a pulse of helpless desperation.

He thought he knew what isolation felt like. But he'd had no idea.

Mother was walking toward him. She'd have some sort of lecture, to be sure. Warranted or not, he'd acted with disgrace this evening. He'd showed the worst of himself in more ways than one. Perhaps sleeping in the barn with Tybalt should be his punishment.

"The air is cold," Mother said, tightening her shawl. "Why don't you come inside? A long night of sleep will do us all some good."

"I am not yet tired," he managed in a low voice. His

mind was not tired, but his legs and feet ached.

"Tomorrow is a fresh day, darling. Caroline will see things clearly."

"She sees everything clearly now, Mother. That is precisely the problem." Preston rubbed his chin. He'd finally gotten what he wanted. Caroline saw what everyone else did: Preston wasn't accepted by Society.

"Her heart has not changed," Mother sighed.

Preston had nothing to say to that. He didn't wish to talk of love with his mother, especially when he was so sure of it slipping through his fingers. What he wanted was to invade Caroline's room and insist she hear him out. He wanted to beg her for another chance to prove himself capable of self-control, of not letting minute things affect him. Especially minute people, like Valcourt.

He *was* capable.

And now more than ever he wanted to make things work between them.

"Do you know how your father proposed marriage to me?" Mother crossed her arms defiantly. Preston shook his head.

"He made a grand gesture." Mother's forehead wrinkled. "His was not a mere declaration of affection. He showed me. So, since you do not wish to speak to your mother about these matters, I will tell you my opinion straight out. If you love Caroline Avery and wish to marry her, show her what you will do to deserve her for the rest of your life. Show her to what end you will go for her happiness."

Preston rubbed his temples. "It is not that simple."

Mother scoffed. "It is always that simple." And with that, she left him.

CHAPTER 9

Caroline slowly pulled her needle up through the handkerchief. A perfect knot stitch for the flower's middle.

She'd told herself upon falling asleep the night before that she would not break her promise to Preston. She could wake from her bed, dress, and sip her tea like any other usual day, and show her face in the drawing room for the morning.

Mama and Mrs. Blake shared pitying looks when she'd entered, but only spared a moment to convey that both Thomas and Preston were out on errands before taking their leave of the room.

Alone, Caroline turned her focus on her stitching instead of wondering what errand would've taken Preston away for the morning. How did he sleep? Was he as disappointed as she?

Drat. She shook her poked finger and rubbed away a mark of blood. Stitching was an awful pastime. She'd just determined to set aside her things when quick footsteps approached from the hallway.

Voices murmured from outside, a shuffling of feet and a laugh.

Caroline turned back to her stitching. Could it be Valcourt, coming for her again? He would have some nerve after his behavior last night. There was a very real possibility she'd land him a facer herself if given the chance. Perhaps she should've a long time ago.

The sound of heavy boots paced toward her. How very rude to enter without being announced. She lifted her head to see who had the audacity to disturb her and pricked her finger again.

"Good morning," Preston said, craning his neck around a rather large basket.

Caroline's hands were raised in midair clutching the cloth she stitched.

Undisturbed by her silence, Preston lowered the giant basket down upon the ground in front of her. It was filled to the brim with small packages. "I'd almost forgotten how busy the market is in the mornings." Preston let out a breath as though he'd overexerted himself. His lip was bruised and slightly swollen from last night's brawl. But he was smiling.

"What is this?" Caroline managed on a whisper. Was it really so easy for him to move on, to be happy again?

"I've been to town," Preston announced like the admission were something to be as acclaimed as winning a first-place trophy. "And I've brought you some things."

Caroline unfurled her brow. Preston had been to *town*? Before she could form a coherent thought, he was on his knees shuffling through the basket.

"This," he said, unwrapping a circular tube and handing it to her. "Should help you with your sketches. Mr. Brown's sundry's store was quite nice, and his assistant very amiable in helping me pick just the right charcoal sticks for your work."

Placing her stitching down beside her, Caroline took the tube and opened it. Burned sticks for her sketching.

"And these"—Preston pulled out another package—"are the latest colors from London. Quite exquisite silk, if you ask me. The gentleman, Mr. Ernest, was just back from a trip."

"Preston." Caroline shook her head as he handed her five new, beautiful silk ribbons. "What is all of this?"

Preston did not answer as he sifted through the basket, through a dozen or more perfectly wrapped packages. He lined them on the floor in front of her and stood to face her. "I went to town this morning," he said again.

Caroline sighed and stood to match him. "Yes, you've said as much. But whatever for? You hate Society and for good reason."

"I did," Preston admitted, reaching for Caroline's hands. "But I love *you*."

Her mouth dropped at the same time her heart took flight. "What?" she breathed.

"Last night . . . I wanted to tell you. But I ruined everything, and I must beg your forgiveness." Preston moved closer and tears pricked at Caroline's eyes. Could this really be happening? Was he saying what she thought he was? "I will not ever enjoy stares or whispers on my behalf. But being with you. The *happiness* I feel with you beside me, no matter what else stands around me . . . I can breathe again. I feel more like myself *with you* than anywhere else in the world."

Caroline wiped a stray tear from her cheek. She had no idea what to say or do. She had no idea what to *think*.

Preston studied her. His eyes grew worried. "I cannot promise you a perfect life. I am far from a perfect man. But for your happiness, I will give everything I am. I will go to market for you, Caroline Avery." At that, she laughed, fingering the lapels on his coat. "I will attend balls and operas, host the occasional party or dinner as you wish. I am capable of withstanding the worst with you beside me. And I promise you," he paused, kneeling on one knee. "I promise you our lives will be as full as you desire. If you'll have me."

Caroline held her middle. Her heart beat fervently in her chest, near to bursting with joy. A person couldn't dream to be this happy.

Preston took her hand in his, and she realized she hadn't answered him. He was kneeling there with a puzzled look on his face. As though he was concerned for her sanity.

"Stand up," she grinned. "And kiss me already. You know my answer is yes."

Preston let out a breath and immediately stood. He laced one hand around her waist and traced the other around her cheek to her neck.

Their noses touched, and Caroline couldn't breathe. She wrapped her arms around his neck and pulled him closer. "I love you, Preston."

His lips touched hers, gently at first, but he must have felt it too, an explosion of fire, for the kiss pulled them deeper together, sweeter than anything imaginable, and

Preston pulled her flush against him. Her breath came in wisps, and his lips moved across her jaw, along her neck as he moved his hands up and down her back.

She hadn't given a single thought to his scars. She only knew she wanted all of him. After what seemed like quite a while, they found themselves very much intertwined against the pianoforte across the room.

"Are you sure this is worth braving the market?" Caroline teased as Preston adjusted his cravat.

"I am quite sure." Preston gave her a wicked grin. "In fact, I'm feeling rather in the mood for another venture, should every trip end as this."

"You despicable man." Caroline kissed his cheek, lacing her fingers through his. "Won't you go and speak to my father now? I am certain our families are wondering where we are."

Preston stifled a laugh. "He gave me his permission this morning. As did Thomas. Our mothers, on the other hand, would likely appreciate the news."

Preston thumbed the back of Caroline's hand, and he pulled her close for one last kiss. "I was such a fool," he said. "To think that I could live without you."

Caroline leaned into his embrace. "You were not a fool. Only blind, my love. But look at you now."

CHAPTER 10

Preston forced his leaden legs up the stair of the coach, pulling himself through to his seat. He wasn't sad to leave Mayberry Park. He was entirely exhausted. An early ceremony followed by a feast of a breakfast was at last coming to a close. Preston had participated in more conversation than he desired in a week let alone a day.

Caroline held a small basket in her lap and yawned behind a hand. The sun had started its descent in the sky and leaving now guaranteed their arrival at his estate—their estate, actually—before evening grew too late. Neither of them wanted to spend their wedding night at Mayberry Park, and the half days' drive would give them a perfect amount of time to recover.

"I do feel a tad guilty leaving your mother behind," Caroline said, leaning her head on his shoulder. She'd changed out of her gown into a more comfortable muslin. A simple white that suited her.

"Not at all." Preston took her hand in his. "She is

happier than I've seen her in years. She'll follow behind us soon enough."

Caroline gave a contented sigh. "You were extraordinary today. I am sure you are exhausted from all the attention. But thank you for giving me time."

"I made you a promise, didn't I?" Preston kissed her hand. "Besides, it was easy. I merely kept my eyes on England's most beautiful bride."

Ruffling sounded from the basket in Caroline's lap. "There, there," she said as she opened the folded lid on one side.

How he'd let Caroline convince him to bring Tybalt home was beyond him. The man was weak, to be sure. But at least Romeo was partial to the pond at Mayberry Park. Even Caroline saw reason in that regard. *After* he'd promised to allow her visits as often as she wished.

"Tybalt might be more comfortable on the floor," Preston said, raising a brow.

"I suppose you are right." She laid a small blanket on the floor before settling the basket near her feet. Preston pulled her closer, trying to suppress the smile that would reveal his mischievous intentions with his wife.

She sighed and snuggled close.

Preston rapped on the roof of the coach, signaling to the driver to continue onward. With a jolt, they were off.

As the night drew in, the coach darkened save for the lantern, and Caroline fell heavily into sleep beside him. Preston took a drowsy glance at his reflection in the glass window for the thousandth time since his accident. But for the first time, he didn't see angry scars or ugliness defining him.

He saw a man both loved and admired despite his flaws.

And inside, he was more than happy, more than grateful, with his lot in life.

For in that moment, he realized one thing: appearance does not change the heart.

Living does.

~

If you enjoyed this fairy tale retelling, check out the other titles in the Forever After Series:

Maiden in the Tower by Heidi Kimball
Beauty and the Baron, by Joanna Barker
The Captain and Miss Winter, by Sally Britton
The Steadfast Heart by Arlem Hawks

YOU CAN CONNECT with Megan Walker on Facebook, or sign up for her newsletter!

ALSO BY MEGAN WALKER

Lakeshire Park
A Beautiful Love
Her Unexpected Courtship

Titles in the Forever After Retellings:

Beauty and the Baron, by Joanna Barker
The Captain and Miss Winter, by Sally Britton
The Steadfast Heart by Arlem Hawks
A Beautiful Love by Megan Walker
Maiden in the Tower by Heidi Kimball

ABOUT THE AUTHOR

Megan Walker was raised on a berry farm where her imagination took her to times past and worlds away. While earning her degree in Early Childhood Education at Brigham Young University, she married her one true love and started a family. But her imaginings wouldn't leave her alone, so she picked up a pen. And the rest is history. She lives in St. Louis, Missouri, with her husband and three children.

Connect with Megan on Facebook.

Made in the USA
Coppell, TX
23 August 2024